GLIMMER TRAIN STORIES

EDITORS
Susan Burmeister
Linda Davies

ASSISTANT EDITOR
Scott Allie

EDITORIAL ASSISTANT
Florence McMullen

CONSULTING EDITOR
Anne M. Callan

COPY EDITOR
Mark Morris

COVER ILLUSTRATION
Jane Zwinger

STORY ILLUSTRATIONS
Jon Leon

LAST PAGE ILLUSTRATION
Bernard Mulligan, Rep. of Ireland

TYPOGRAPHY/LAYOUT
Paul O. Giesey/Adcrafters

PUBLISHED QUARTERLY
in February, May, August, and November by
Glimmer Train Press, Inc.
812 SW Washington Street, Suite 1205
Portland, Oregon 97205-3216 U.S.A.
Telephone: 503/221-0836
Facsimile: 503/221-0837

Glimmer Train (ISSN #1055-7520) is published quarterly, $29 per year in the U.S., by Glimmer Train Press, Inc., Suite 1205, 812 SW Washington, Portland, OR 97205. Second-class postage paid at Portland, OR, and additional mailing offices. POSTMASTER: Send address changes to Glimmer Train Press, Inc., Suite 1205, 812 SW Washington, Portland, OR 97205.

ISSN # 1055-7520, ISBN # 1-880966-06-9, CPDA BIPAD # 79021

DISTRIBUTION: Bookstores can purchase *Glimmer Train Stories* through these distributors:
Bernhard DeBoer, Inc., 113 E. Centre St., Nutley, NJ 07110
Bookpeople, 7900 Edgewater Dr., Oakland, CA 94621
Ingram Periodicals, 1226 Heil Quaker Blvd., LaVergne, TN 37086
IPD, 674 Via de la Valle, #204, Solana Beach, CA 92075
Pacific Pipeline, 8030 S. 228th St., Kent, WA 98032
Ubiquity, 607 Degraw St., Brooklyn, NY 11217

PRINTED IN U.S.A. ON RECYCLED, ACID-FREE PAPER. ♺

Subscription rates: One year, $29 within the U.S. (Visa/MC/check).
Airmail to Canada, $39; outside North America, $49.
Payable by Visa/MC or check for U.S. dollars drawn on a U.S. bank.

*Attention short-story writers: We pay $300 for first publication and one-time anthology rights. Please include a self-addressed, sufficiently stamped envelope with your submission. **Manuscripts accepted in January, April, July, and October.** Send a SASE for guidelines.*

Dedication

The sum of all we have ever read
is a mammoth force in our lives.

Feather strokes from thousands and thousands of turning pages
lace our hands, mark us.
We'll never be the same again.

We emerge from final paragraphs, and we are a bit new.
Sometimes we feel the feather strokes as thin cuts,
our hands tender having seen something fresh.

And sometimes we see that an old ache is eased,
fingers flexed, palms cooler,
hands steadied, having finally understood.
The feathers work their magic.

We read, and we are changed.
We dedicate this issue to the pages that have changed us.

Susan Burmeister   Linda Davis

$\mathscr{C}$ONTENTS

Liz Szabla
Dearborn
7

Joyce Thompson
First Out
19

Joyce Carol Oates
The Missing Person
33

Interview with Doris Lessing
Voice of England, voice of Africa
50

Kiran Kaur Saini
A Girl Like Elsie
65

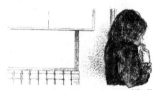

Roxana Robinson
Sleepover
81

Article by Siobhan Dowd
Writer Detained: Ren Wanding
92

Richard Bausch
The Natural Effects of Divorce
97

CONTENTS

Stewart David Ikeda
Roughie
119

Katherine Min
Objects
125

Stephen Dixon
Interstate 3, Paragraph 2
135

Interview with Linda Hornbuckle
Blues singer
142

Susan Burmeister
The Two-Step
154

Stories Gone By
Past issues outline
158

What do they have going now?
Coming this fall
160

Liz Szabla

*I think it was ducks in a pond that had me so mesmerized.
I still like animal crackers.*

Liz Szabla was a writer-in-residence last fall at the Syvenna Foundation in Linden, Texas, where, among other work, she finished writing "Dearborn."

Szabla was born and raised in San Francisco, moved to New York City in 1984, and now lives in Hoboken, New Jersey.

LIZ SZABLA
Dearborn

rank stood behind the counter of Big Leo's store, shifting his weight from one foot to the other, his elbows resting among the jars of licorice and jawbreakers and peppermints. He had managed to clear enough space to prop a book open before him. He pulled a cigarette from the package in his breast pocket and tamped one end on the counter as he read.

Outside, the bells of St. Theresa's rang in the three o'clock mass. Frank lit the cigarette and tossed the match into an old coffee can on the shelf below the cash register. He'd been in the store since seven and had yet to make a sale. He glanced through the window at the gray February sky and then went back to reading. His father insisted on staying open Sundays, even though Saturday was when most of the customers picked up their orders of kielbasa and babka for Sunday dinner. The war had changed things. Big Leo explained to Frank that if a family hadn't picked up an order by closing time on Saturday, it meant a telegram had come. Telegrams meant that people bought a little extra—some coffee and sugar, cakes to serve after mass each day while waiting for the son to be shipped home. Big Leo said business was bound to get better on Sundays. Frank sometimes noticed him standing at the door during the week, smoking and looking up Porath Street for the Western Union man. It was always a shame, Big Leo said, to lose another of the neighbor-hood boys.

Sundays. Every Sunday Frank checked the storeroom in the basement to see who hadn't picked up their orders. The Sunday before Christmas it had been John Buchinski's family. John, and Frank's brother Eddie, were gunners in the same Air Force division, different squads. The last anyone had heard, they were both stationed in Italy. The family sent John's little sister Edith to pick up the food. She had kept her eyes lowered as Frank wrapped a thick slice of ham in white paper.

"My ma didn't give me money for that," she whispered.

Frank added the ham to the bundle of sausage and bread. He noticed that Edith had buttoned her overcoat wrong, the first button in the second buttonhole.

"Tell her it's from our family to yours. Tell her we'll pray for you," he said. After Edith left, he wiped the butcher knife clean and put it back in the basement where Big Leo did the slaughtering.

Frank looked up from his book. He thought he heard someone coming, but it was only the wind rattling the door on its hinges. There was talk of a blizzard. He listened for a moment longer while he finished his cigarette. The clock on the wall behind him ticked softly. His mother was quiet upstairs. Frank hoped she was resting. A stroke ten years before had left one side of her dead, a clean line cut through the middle of her. Sunday was the only day she didn't have to look after Big Leo. On Sundays, he played cards all day in Tony Stassa's basement. Frank thought about locking the door and going upstairs to read, but it would upset his mother. She'd spend the afternoon worrying that Big Leo might come home early, though he had never been home before five for as long as Frank could remember. Sundays went by faster when Eddie was there. They could talk, or take turns going upstairs to sit down and drink a cup of coffee. There were no chairs in the store. Big Leo did not allow his boys to sit down on the job. He said it looked bad to customers to see his stupid polack sons sitting on their fat polack asses. Frank and Eddie slouched and leaned against the counter, they smoked and made sandwiches, but they never sat down. Big Leo's boys did as they were told.

Frank rubbed his eyes and closed the book, marking his place with a pencil. He lifted the lid from the jar of licorice and pulled a piece out. He thought of Eddie flying maneuvers somewhere over Italy. Upstairs was a snapshot of Eddie and a couple of buddies leaning against their plane. Eddie's arms were folded in front of his chest. He was looking into the sun and smiling widely. On the back of the photograph, he had written, "Me in Italy October 12, 1943." Eddie had been gone almost a year. He didn't write much, and when a letter came, Big Leo made Frank read it to him several times before it was folded back up and slipped between the pages of the heavy black Bible. In one of the letters, Eddie wrote, "Frank—don't read this to Ma and Pa. I wish you could see the Girls here. They are something else!!" Frank thought about beautiful dark-haired girls with lips painted red as blood. He and Eddie had enlisted together, but after three physicals, Frank was let go. The doctors said he had a heart murmur. He was seventeen. It was the first he'd heard about it. Eddie slapped him on the back and told him not to take it too hard.

The same month Eddie shipped out overseas from North Carolina, Frank began his freshman year across town at Wayne State. If it weren't for the scholarship that paid his tuition, and a stipend for books, he might not have gone. He didn't know anyone there; all the boys he knew were in the service. On the first day of school, Big Leo had watched from behind the counter as Frank reached for a pack of cigarettes. He caught Frank's hand in his own huge fist.

"You got work right here," he said. "You got a responsibility to the store."

Big Leo held onto him a second more. Frank avoided his father's burning eyes and focused instead on his hard chin, dotted with black and white stubble. From then on, before he left in the morning, Frank prepared the meat for the kielbasa, or cleaned chickens in the old enamel bathtub in the basement. The smell stayed with him all day. In between classes he stood in the hallway and smoked.

Frank lit another cigarette and picked licorice from his teeth. It was the time of day when most of the neighborhood was sitting down to Sunday dinner. He suddenly felt cold and remembered the furnace. A draft in the basement had probably blown out the flame. He flipped on the light to the basement. He had gotten so tall he had to duck to keep from bumping his head as he went down the stairs.

The basement was raw, the dirt floors dank. The walls were lined with sagging wooden shelves, which held neat rows of bottles and cans. The old bathtub rested against the wall across from the furnace and coal bin. Frank walked over to it and peered inside to check for mice. Years of butchering had stained its sides the color of wine. Before his mother's stroke, when she could still come downstairs, Frank had helped her collect the blood from chickens and ducks for soup. He had to lean over the tub and hold the bodies close while his mother cut the necks and steadied them so the blood emptied into the bowl she placed beneath the wound. She sang softly in Polish while Frank dug his fingers in the birds' soft breasts to keep them from struggling.

The furnace was quiet. Frank thought of his mother upstairs. She wouldn't complain even if she were cold. She rarely spoke above a whisper, as if the stroke had frozen half her voice. The one side of her was always cold when he carried her up and down the stairs, but she couldn't feel it. It had happened when she was forty-six. The doctor told Eddie she'd had another miscarriage.

He shoveled coal into the furnace and lit it, squatting to warm his hands and face. The basement smelled like meat and earth and fear. The smell was as familiar to Frank as his skin. He inhaled deeply and patted his shirt for cigarettes.

In the middle of the basement stood a wooden post. Its splintering sides were squared into four sharp corners, which stretched from floor to ceiling. The post was dry, solid as trees. Frank stood and dragged a match across one side until it sparked, then dropped it to the ground and watched it die. When they were younger, Big Leo had told Frank and Eddie that the post held the store and the whole house up, that the slightest pressure against it might send the building crashing down on their heads. Even though he knew better, Frank still thought about one day laying all his strength against the post, maybe get Eddie to join in, and see what happened.

He heard the door open and close upstairs. Someone took two steps inside and yelled, "Hello! Is anyone there?"

Frank ran up the steps and into the store, leaving the basement door open behind him. The man was facing away. He wore a cap like a policeman's.

"Can I help you?"

"Hope so," the man said as he turned. The brim of his cap had the Western Union insignia on it. "I sure would like it if you had somethin' hot to drink, and maybe a roll, if you still have any."

"There's coffee hot upstairs," Frank said. "I'll be right back."

He took the stairs three at a time. His mother was quiet in her room. He wrapped a dishrag around the handle of the coffeepot and lifted it from the stove. When he got back downstairs, he reached behind the counter for a cup.

"Anything in it?" he asked the man.

"Nope, just black's how I like it."

Frank poured the coffee and made some room on one of the shelves to set the pot down. He tossed the dishrag over one

J. LEON 93

shoulder. The man took the cup and held it under his nose.

"Now this is more like it," he said. "It's cold as hell out there today."

"I didn't know you boys worked on Sundays," Frank said.

"Sundays, Saturdays. They're keepin' us busy."

"You want a sandwich or something?"

"Well sure, that'd be fine, but I need to count my change here ..." The man started to reach into his pocket.

"No charge," Frank said. "On the house."

He walked behind the counter to a case with two yellow rounds of cheese. He put a wedge of cheese and a loaf of brown bread on the butcher block and cut two slices from each.

"Butter?" he asked.

"If you can spare it," the man said.

"So what brings you to Porath Street?" Frank asked without looking up.

"I just came down from Hamtramck. Had three fellas' families to deliver to." The man took a sip of the coffee.

"Hey, this is good," he said. "So I got one more in my pocket for Dearborn. I'm thinkin', maybe I'll just head home. I live out in Melvindale, you know it? Dearborn's on my way. But I'm thinkin', these folks don't need to hear about their boy on Sunday, why not let it wait till tomorrow. Then I remember about that blizzard, and if it shuts us down there's no tellin' how long we'll be out. I'm tellin' you, after you done this for a while, all them boys become like your own, you know what I mean?"

Frank nodded and handed him the sandwich.

"Thanks much." The man scanned the store for a place to sit down. After a moment, he shrugged his shoulders and set the cup down on the nearest shelf. He grasped the sandwich in both hands and took a great bite. "Good," he said through the food.

Frank came back around the counter and poured more coffee into the man's cup. The man ate noisily, licking the crumbs from his fingers. Frank looked at the clock. Four-thirty. It was starting to get dark outside. He hoped the man would leave before Big Leo got back.

"What's the place you're trying to find?" he asked. "Maybe I can give you directions."

The man took a long swallow of coffee.

"Thanks anyway, kid, but we're not authorized to give out names," he said. "Don't worry about me, I been through this neighborhood before. You grow up here?"

Frank nodded. He could feel his pulse in his temples.

"This your pa's store? Mighty tough business to be in, times like these."

"We've been here a long time," Frank said.

"Got lots of customers, do ya?" The man looked around the store. He reached inside his coat and pulled out a pack of cigarettes. "Kind of slow now, though. How come you're open Sunday?"

"Someone might need something." Frank handed the man a light.

"Like me, I s'pose."

Frank wondered if the man was going to ask him why he wasn't in the service. He usually answered "bum ticker" and then hoped the person asking didn't think he was lying to look at him, big and thick-armed, lifting sacks of flour like they were pillows.

"Got anyone overseas?" the man asked.

"My brother."

"What division?"

"Air," Frank said.

The man walked over to a shelf, picked up a bottle of ketchup, wiped his finger over the lid. It came up clean. He put the bottle back down.

"Brave boy. Air's got it bad over there. Got any gum?" He walked back to the counter and picked up the book Frank had left between the jars of candy. "Yours?"

"Yeah, it's mine." Frank took a piece of spearmint gum from one of the jars. He wondered when the man would leave.

"*Walden*. Hmmm. I think I heard of this." He opened the book to where Frank had marked his place with the pencil. "You're almost done with it. You in school?"

"Wayne State." Frank took the dishrag from his shoulder and wiped the butcher block. "Say, mister, do you want more coffee or anything?"

The man looked up from the book and squinted at Frank through the smoke from his cigarette. He put it back on the counter.

"No thanks, son. What do I owe ya?"

"Fifteen cents for the coffee, penny for the gum."

"Here's a quarter, keep the change." The man put the coin on the counter and dropped his cigarette in the coffee cup. "Much obliged for the sandwich. It's a hell of a day to be workin', know what I mean?"

The man touched the brim of his cap and turned toward the door. He paused for a moment and turned back to Frank.

"You and your pa make kielbasi, don't ya?"

Frank nodded.

"Thought so," the man said. "Smells real good in here. Like Sunday dinner's cookin'. I have to remember this place, so's I can come back sometime and get an order."

"Thanks," Frank said.

Big Leo walked into the store at ten past five. His worn felt hat was dusted with new snow. He locked the door behind him and turned the sign in the glass around so the side that read "Closed" faced the street.

Frank was standing behind the counter reading. The door startled him. Big Leo walked over to the cash register and rang the till open.

"How much?" he said.

Frank could smell the liquor on him. Sundays had never been churchgoing days for Big Leo. He and his group played cards for money.

"Quarter. For coffee," Frank said.

Big Leo slammed the till shut, rattling some of the candy jars. Frank noticed that the top button of his father's shirt was cutting into the flesh at his throat. Big Leo looked down at the book and snatched it from Frank's hands.

"Is this what you do when you work for me?" he yelled, his breath hitting Frank like fire. "Goddammit! Is this what you do all day?"

"Pa," Frank said, "I swept, and cleaned up the case. No one came in but a man looking to warm up . . ."

Big Leo threw the book across the room. It knocked a box of baking soda off a shelf before it landed facedown on the floor, its pages spread to either side like arms.

"Pa," Frank said. "It was slow."

Big Leo strode around the store, his big black shoes leaving wet prints on the old wood floor.

"You got no work? You finish your work?" he cried. He stopped in front of a couple bushels of potatoes piled high in an open crate they kept next to the onions. Frank watched the old man bend over and hoist the crate to his chest with the strength of a bear. He carried it to the top of the basement stairs, to the door that Frank had left open.

"You want something to do?" Big Leo heaved the crate down the stairs. The potatoes pounded down the hollow wood steps like rocks. Frank stared at the coffeepot he'd left out. He thought of his mother upstairs in her room listening to Big Leo and covering her face. He wanted to go pick up the book.

Big Leo walked slowly to the counter and stood before Frank.

"You're not finished working yet," he said. "Now you have something to do."

Frank waited until his father was upstairs to come out from

16

behind the counter. He picked up the book, a page fluttered to the floor. He slipped it inside the front cover. He carried the book down to the basement, stepping around a few potatoes that had lodged on the stairs. The furnace glowed in the corner. He walked over to the post, cleared a place on the floor, and sat down on the smooth dirt. He reached above him and struck a match against the wood. He leaned back and smoked, remembering how quietly he and Eddie had sat in the dark, not even daring to reach for each other, when Big Leo had tied them to the post and told them not to move or the house would fall down.

Joyce Thompson

Want to see my bubble?

*(I don't remember any of this except the lamp and the
radiator. I kind of like it, though. Nice legs, huh?)*

Joyce Thompson describes her present position as "that grandiose and paranoid
territory between finishing one novel and committing to the next." She is
cleaning her house, answering letters, and taking long walks on the beach.

Joyce Thompson (signature)

JOYCE THOMPSON
First Out

I suppose you might say this all happened because I didn't listen to what my friend Ted said after I announced to him one day I believed I was ready to be somebody's first lover out. Ted laughed in my face.

The recently estranged are ten percent personality, ninety percent grievance, Ted said. All they talk about is lawyers. All they think about is themselves. Besides, Ted said, whoever heard of anybody ending up with their first one out? It's statistically improbable, to say the least.

I know that, Ted, I said. But listen up. I said lover, not lifemate.

Ted and I met a couple of years back, when I'd been divorced about five years and Ted was still waiting for his decree. A powerful attraction, abetted by half a bottle of red wine, carried us right to the brink of becoming lovers ourselves, but then common sense somehow got the upper hand, before anything you might call irreversible had taken place.

I'd cut my leg with a recalcitrant chain saw not long before, and Ted and I struck a deal, perhaps as consolation: When my scar disappeared (an outward and visible symbol), his heart would be healed (by a mysterious and inexorable psychic/organic process), and we could then, if we chose, reopen

Glimmer Train Stories, Issue 7, Summer 1993
©*1993 Joyce Thompson*

negotiations about the lover thing. The tooth marks on my ankle have been invisible for at least a year now, but neither one of us has chosen to broach the subject of Eros. My current relationship with Ted is probably most accurately described in terms of what it isn't. We are, I think, true friends.

The word is masochist, Lizzie, Ted said. There are no exceptions to this particular rule. Remember Candy?

How could I forget Candy, I said.

Being friends has not dwindled our mutual attraction, just turned it in some strange directions. Instead of doing, we tell. We tell each other everything about our little flirtations and affairs, which is both painful and titillating, often at the same time.

Ted sighed. It was that body, he said. It was at least the hundredth time I'd heard him say that. His eyes narrow and defocus when he thinks about Candy's body. Those hips, Ted said. Those breasts.

While my feminist influence has failed to cure Ted entirely of the male sin of viewing certain females as what he refers to as "sack fodder," I have educated the coarser synonyms for "breast" out of his working vocabulary, at least when he's talking to me or members of my immediate family. Candy not only turned Ted into a fool, she made him miserable besides. If I were to be completely honest, I would probably have to say I was a little bit jealous of her.

Do what you want, though, Ted said. I suppose you have someone in mind?

Actually, I'm still in the conceptual stages, I told him. Do you happen to know any attractive, recently divorced men?

None I'd introduce you to, Ted said.

Why not? I said.

They're all fucked up. If you're going to be somebody's shrink, you should at least get paid for it.

I was thinking of myself more as a sister of mercy, I said.

20

Besides, everyone has fond memories of their first lover out.

Let me get this straight, Ted said, with that sideways tilt of his head. You aspire to become the fond memory of some man you haven't even met yet?

Actually, Ted, I said, I just want to get laid.

Ted shook his head emphatically enough so that the ponytail he's taken to wearing to compensate for his early baldness waggled at me. And I suppose you expect me to offer you diet Coke and sympathy when you suffer the inevitable slings and arrows of ignoring my advice?

You can have diet if you want, Ted, I said. I'll take the real thing.

That's what we all want—the real thing—even though most of us don't have the slightest notion of what that is. We tell ourselves we'll know it if and when it happens along; in my case, it's a brilliant hunk who is kind and sensuous and willing to love both me and my children. Ted, I think, is holding out for a love goddess with a Ph.D. Sometimes I wonder if we don't set our sights so high to spare ourselves the trouble of actually trying to get along, romantically speaking, with an imperfect fellow human.

The good news is, sometime following my fortieth birthday, it occurred to me that the real thing and getting laid are neither synonymous nor mutually exclusive. Men seem to understand that innately, from the time they reach puberty, but for a woman of a certain age, it is a liberating revelation. You may be single for the rest of your natural life, but that doesn't have to mean you're going to die celibate. Maybe this only seems like good news after you've parted company with the better part of your illusions, like the one about having more babies someday, or that age is somehow going to make an exception in your case. I don't know.

Anyway, I was getting pretty tired of waiting passively for the real thing to find me, so I decided to act upon this liberating revelation without delay. The first thing I had to do, of course, was find a man. Once you stop looking for the real thing and start smiling more or less indiscriminately at lesser mortals, things start to happen. Cups of coffee and walks, movies, dinner. My kids noticed, of course, and didn't much like it; they hadn't really had to share me with anybody else for a long time, except Ted, whom they had come to accept as a friend of the family. I couldn't tell my children I was looking to get laid, so when Manda asked me, What is going on here, Mom? I shrugged innocently and said, You kids are growing up. It's time I had more of a social life, is all.

For a couple of months, I auditioned a good number of men of all shapes and sizes and persuasions, without finding a suitable candidate; I do have standards, after all, or maybe they're nothing more than prejudices. Still, they're mine and I respect them. No married men, of course. No short men. No fat men. No Republicans or evangelicals. No heavy drinkers or druggies. Nobody too much older or too much younger than me. Nobody too rich or too poor or too eager to get married. These standards evolved over time, based on experience.

Ted and I didn't see much of each other during that stretch— we were both busy with work, and he was dating a fair amount himself—but, every now and then, he'd call me up to see how it was going, or, as he said one day, Hey, Lizzie, you found one of the walking wounded yet?

Assorted cripples, I told him, but nobody I'd trust to recover. How about you?

Keeping busy, he said. Hey, maybe you should read the dissolutions column in the paper. There's at least a couple dozen new prospects every week.

Good idea, I said.

I was kidding, Ted said.

So was I. Actually, I'm getting a little discouraged. This dating stuff is pretty time-consuming. Half the time, I'd rather be home playing canasta with the kids.

Then I heard the double thunk on the line that meant Ted had another call. Want me to put you on hold, Ted said, or say good-bye?

Good-bye, I said. Grateful as I was to have Ted in the wings with his diet Coke, waiting to sweep up the pieces, I understood this was a mission I had to undertake alone.

I had the notion I would encounter my candidate while I was working; that's when I meet the most new people. But one day, toward the end of November, I took my son Josh to one of the local television studios where they were taping a Christmas special. Josh sings in a children's choir. Neither Manda nor I can carry a tune across the street, but Josh has a lovely voice and he likes to perform. Dozens of us stage mothers were standing around, proud and a little stupid, while they herded our junior choristers around the stage set and tuned them up. Then I heard a voice ask, Who's the kid in the blue sweater who sings the solo in "Silent Night"?

I raised my hand. That's my son Josh, I said.

The voice belonged to a man with a clipboard. Spell the last name, please, he said.

As I spelled, I couldn't help noticing what nice blue eyes the man had.

Cute kid, the man said. You must be proud.

Thanks. I am. His big sister would rather he was a second baseman, not a boy soprano, though. Siblings, I said.

Women, the man said. He had a good thick moustache, no beard, and plenty of brown-blond hair.

Oh, we're not so bad, I said.

The man looked at me, not as Josh's mother, and smiled. He shifted the clipboard into his left hand and held out his right. I'm Jake Riddell, he said. I used to produce the five o'clock news, but Wayne didn't like me, so now I'm doing public-service crap.

Oh, I said. Should I be sorry?

It's all part of the game, Jake said. You got a name?

Elizabeth, I said, but no one calls me that. I'm Liz, or Lizzie.

Glad to meet you, Liz. Jake took up his pen again. Now, what's Josh's phone number, please?

What do you want that for? I said. You going to offer him a job?

Jake actually blushed a little. I was thinking of calling his mother sometime, he said. You think she'd mind?

I gave him Josh's number.

By the time the special aired three weeks later, Josh's mother and Jake, the producer of public-service crap, had spent a fair amount of time getting to know each other. He'd looked at my photographs and met my kids. I'd heard the grisly details, some, at least; Wayne the anchorman and Lucy the estranged wife, a former weathergirl, had turned on Jake at just about the same time, four months before, which was more recently than even I would have wished. True, his first affair out still lay before him, but he was strapped tight to the emotional roller coaster yet, riding a cycle at whose height he was a pleasant, animated companion, and in whose depth, a self-pitying, egomaniacal bore. Unfortunately, it was impossible to predict which man I would be seeing on any given occasion.

Maybe because Jake was by far the most promising specimen I'd yet unearthed, I chose to see this as the downside of my experiment. After all, anyone of us who has passed through the valley of the shadow of divorce was once a miserable sniveling wreck herself, sustained by the kindness of tolerant souls; I kept reminding myself that Jake deserved his turn. At his best, he was articulate and amusing. He swam and cycled regularly, so his body, if a little on the thin side, was nothing to sneeze at. I liked him, without feeling the slightest temptation to fall in love with him. In short, he was as close to ideal as a woman in search of compromise was likely to come. I was prepared to be kind and tolerant.

As it turned out, we became lovers on one of those nights the roller coaster was riding low. Jake was full of lawyer-venom, interspersed with frequent reproaches of the gods, because of some official papers the process server had laid on him earlier that day. I tried to look alert as the sorry tale spilled out. When Jake paused long enough in his catalogue of sorrows for me to speak, what I said was, Do you need a hug?

Oh yes, Jake said.

We were sitting side by side on his sofa. I slung my arm across his shoulders and squeezed. Quick as a flash, Jake got both arms around me, pulled me close and kissed me, one of those long movie kisses that start chaste and then, by lingering degrees, turn passionate, a waking-up kiss that slowly rouses all those parts of you that have been sleeping, a kiss with consequences. At the end of a kiss like that, the question has been asked and answered. Unless the building you're in catches fire or the ship you're sailing sinks, there is no turning back.

We didn't turn back. The first time, you might say, was for him, more flattering than satisfactory to me, but Jake had been hungry so long his appetite soon revived, and then more than my ego was fed. Nothing bumped up against my soul or quite silenced my mind, but I had gotten what I was after, and I was glad. Jake was grateful. He said some nice things about my legs and my hair and various other parts of me. I remembered how much the recently separated are in need of reassurance, and said quite a few nice things about him.

The next day, since I enjoy being right almost as much as I like getting laid, I called up Ted and told him my good news.

That's nice, Lizzie, Ted said.

Nice? I said. If you don't say you're happy for me, I'll tell the IRS your trip to Hawaii last February was not a legitimate business expense.

I'm happy for you, Lizzie, Ted said. May all your hormones do the hoochie-koochie dance.

No sour grapes?

Of course not, Ted said. I hope you get everything you want.

I don't really want much, Ted, I said.

The affair continued more than it progressed, which was just fine with me. In the years since my divorce, all of my lovers had been chosen rather specifically for their geographic undesirability, a way to keep my amorous adventures from impinging on the lives of my children, so sleeping with a man who lived twenty minutes away, if the freeway was clear, was a new experience. I found myself much more receptive to Jake's laments once I knew they would not be the evening's only form of entertainment, his lows more tolerable once I knew that I had the power to lift him out of them. Jake seemed energized. He put on a little weight and the pain in his back disappeared. I suppose, looking back, it was no more than okay, but at the time and for a while, it was very much okay.

My daughter Manda is a newly minted woman. Another four inches, and she'll be taller than me, which, the way she is growing, should take her all of six months. At least for now, she is both slight and ripe. Her breasts are already bigger than mine. The new shapes her body is assuming make her think she has a right to be privy to previously forbidden territories of her mother's life. One Saturday night, when Josh was spending the night with a friend, and Manda and I were eating a leisurely dinner in front of the fire, she said, So, Mom, are you in love with Jake?

Nope, I said.

Has he kissed you yet? she said.

My daughter looked curious and sympathetic and very young. I smiled at her.

That means he has, she said. Has he French-kissed you yet?
Come on, Manda.

I tell you everything, she said.

French kissing is no big deal, I said.

For me it is. I wouldn't French-kiss anybody I wasn't in love
with.

Good, I said. But it's a little different for grown-ups.

Why? she said.

You'll see.

Manda grinned. She spoke in the same wheedling and defiant
tone she uses to get me to give her money or permission against
my better judgment. I don't want to see, she said, I want you to
tell me.

Her big blue eyes, with their long black lashes, were avid-
bright. The firelight made her pale skin look like pure gold. How
much I want it to be new and sweet for her when her time
comes, every nuance delicious and rare. I chose my words
carefully, so as not to take any of that away. We expect less, I told

her, hoping she would forget that until she needed to remember.

The next weekend, when my children were visiting their father, I spent Friday night with Jake and all day Saturday and Saturday night in the darkroom, printing. Jake had invited me to his place for Sunday breakfast. I brought a pineapple. After he let me in, he kissed me lightly on the cheek. Get a lot done? he asked.

Uh-huh, I said. I'm all caught up. I even—

I had a bad night, Jake said. Lucy called. She wanted to talk about the settlement.

Too bad, I said. Remember I told you I wanted to try some superimposition? Well, I took—

She was all business, Jake said. Dollars and cents. No way you would have guessed we lived together for nine good years.

Sometimes it's too hard to remember the good stuff, I said. Want me to cut up the pineapple?

Sure, Jake said. He hovered in the kitchen while I did. Lucy expects me to support her until she can get a decent job, Jake said. But she's too old to be a weathergirl. She wants me to pay the bills while she gets a master's degree in art history.

How about getting me a bowl to put this in, I said.

Art history, for God's sake, Jake said. What kind of job's she going to get with that?

I arranged the pineapple pieces in the bowl he gave me. Maybe she could teach, I said.

Sure, Jake said. Only Lucy doesn't like kids. That's why we never had any.

You told me that, I said.

I wanted kids, Jake said. She waited until after we were married to tell me she didn't.

Right, I said. The cinnamon rolls should be warm by now. It's time to eat.

Jake set the table. I poured the coffee and served the food. We sat and filled our plates. Jake buttered his cinnamon roll. I should warn you, Lizzie, I don't feel like making love today.

Fine, I said. Please pass the butter when you're done.

I'm too depressed, Jake said.

I understand.

Just because you're having an affair, you don't always have to make love, right? he said.

Right, I said. How about that butter?

Jake passed me the butter. Lucy says she always liked art better than weather. It's news to me.

I thought about a hawk soaring inside a fishbowl, one of the pictures I'd made the night before. Maybe it was a cheap trick, but I liked the image. People change, I said.

I wonder, Jake said. It makes me wonder if I ever knew her in the first place. I mean, how could she—

Good breakfast, Jake, I said. I'll just help you clean up and then I've got to—

Don't go, Liz, Jake said. Please.

After breakfast, we sat on the sofa. I half listened while Jake talked about Lucy some more. With the other part of my mind, I thought about my work. I'd always resisted superimposing images before because the results were too likely to be cute, or low-rent surrealism, which is pretty much the same thing. As I sat there, though, I started thinking about how patterns recur in nature, how I could show that, and the pictures I imagined were beautiful and subtle. When Jake said, I said, I could sure use a hug, I realized how much I had not been listening.

I hugged Jake. Jake kissed me. After a while he said, I guess I was wrong, about not wanting to make love, so we went into his bedroom and took off our clothes, but we did not make love. Instead, we did something rough and hasty and almost angry. I wanted to be in my darkroom. It was over in minutes. Oh well, I thought. Then Jake began to cry.

I thought about mercy and stroked his hair. Jake sobbed. His face across the pillow was ugly with his pain. His crying frightened me. I thought about my children. When they cry, my heart goes out to them, I feel their pain. I could not feel Jake's pain, only watch it. Watching, I almost wished I loved him, but I didn't. Mercy. I made myself be gentle, stroking.

Jake said, I thought about her. Half the time we make love, I'm thinking about her. Part of me still loves her, Liz.

I stroked Jake's hair and murmured consolations, but I realized my heart was breaking, too, not because what Jake said hurt me, but because suddenly I saw my children's father and his pain, pain I had caused, but never felt. I had my own pain then. Now I felt his. Jake gave it to me, but it was not Jake's fault.

I got up and put on my clothes, then sat down on the edge of the bed and touched Jake lightly on the back. I said, I'm sorry, but I have to go now. Jake nodded.

I left, but I couldn't leave the hurt behind. It followed me home, into the darkroom, and made my hands shake so hard I couldn't work. I made myself a pot of tea. I turned on the television and offered myself up to the Sunday afternoon movie, but it wouldn't take me. I called Ted and got his machine. Finally, I sat down at my desk and wrote a letter to my children's father. I asked him to forgive me, not for leaving, but for causing him pain. I sealed the letter in an envelope, wrote his name on the front, and tacked the letter to the front door, where he'd be sure to find it when he brought the children home. And then I cried.

I was still crying when the kids got home. They found me sitting on the sofa in the dark. I was glad to see them; I wiped my eyes and smiled. They climbed up on the sofa with me, Josh on one side and Manda on the other. Did you hurt yourself, Mommy? Josh asked me. I shook my head no.

What's wrong, Mom? Manda said.

I'm sad, is all.

Did you break up with Jake?

Uh-uh.

What is it, then?

I couldn't tell my children what was wrong without making them much older than they were. Instead, I asked them, Did your father find the letter on the door?

He found it, but he didn't open it, Manda said. He took it with him.

Good, I said. He needs to read it by himself.

My children are the enemy of sadness. Josh asked if he could tickle me. I told him sure. After a while, Manda set aside her new sophistication and joined us in the free-for-all. We tickled and wrestled and hugged each other for a long time, until Manda said, I'm hungry, and Josh said, Me too, and I realized that so was I.

I took them out for pizza. When we got back, the light on the answering machine was blinking. I assumed it was Ted, calling me back, but when I played the message, the voice I heard belonged to the father of my children, the man I had lived with and tried to love for thirteen years.

I forgive you, Lizzie, is all he said.

We have no photo available.

Joyce Carol Oates

Joyce Carol Oates is the author most recently of the novel *Black Water* (Dutton) and the story collection *Where Is Here?* (Ecco). Her forthcoming novel is *Foxfire: Confessions of a Girl Gang* (Dutton).

Oates lives in Princeton, New Jersey, where she is on the faculty of Princeton University.

Joyce Carol Oates

JOYCE CAROL OATES
The Missing Person

*H*is name was Robert, and he was not the sort of man you'd feel comfortable calling Bob, still less Bobbie, or Rob. He was tall, not large-boned but densely, solidly built, an athlete in school, now years ago, but retaining his athlete's sense of himself as a distinct physical presence; the kind of man who, shaking your hand, looks you directly in the eye as if he's already your friend—or hopes to be. In his own mind, he moved through the world—now easily, now combatively—as if he had no name, no definition, at all.

He'd fallen in love with the woman before he learned her name, and even after he learned her name, and they'd become in fact lovers, he couldn't deceive himself that he knew her, really. And sometimes this made him very angry, and sometimes it did not.

He was thirty-six years old, which is not young. He'd been married, and a father, and divorced, by the time he was twenty-nine.

He told himself, I can't wait.

One April evening, when Ursula had been away for nearly two weeks, without having told Robert where she was going, or even that she was going away, he turned onto her street,

Glimmer Train Stories, Issue 7, Summer 1993
©*1993 Joyce Carol Oates*

driving aimlessly, and he saw, passing the small wood-frame house she rented, that she was back: lights were burning upstairs and down, her car was in the drive. It had been raining lightly most of the day, and there was a gauzy, dreamy, scrimlike texture to the air. Robert told himself, It's all right, of course it's all right, behave like any friend since you *are* the woman's friend, and not an adversary. He was shaky, but he wasn't upset, and he didn't believe he was angry. That phase of his life—being possessive of a woman, intruding where, for all his manly attractiveness, he wasn't always welcome—was forever ended.

So she was home, and she hadn't so much as told him she was going to be away, but he was in love with her, so it was all right, what she did had to be all right since he loved her—wasn't there logic here? And, if not logic, simple common sense?

The important thing was, she *was* back, in that house. And, so far as Robert could judge—he could see her moving about, through the carelessly drawn venetian blinds at her front windows—she was alone.

So he parked his car, walked unhesitatingly up to the door, rang the doorbell, smiling, seemingly at ease, rehearsing a few words to take the edge off his anxiety (just happened to be driving by, saw your lights), and, when Ursula opened the door, throwing it back in that characteristic way of hers in which she did most things, with an air of welcome, of curiosity, of abandon, of recklessness, yet also of resignation, and he saw her face, he saw her eyes, what shone startled and unfeigned in her eyes, he thought, she *is* the one.

Not long afterward, upstairs, in her bedroom, in her bed, Ursula said accusingly, though also teasingly, "Hey. I know you."

"Yes?"

"You're the one who wants me to love you. So that you won't have to love *me*."

Robert laughed uneasily. "What's that—a riddle?"

It was the first time the word, that word, *love*, had passed between them.

Ursula laughed too. "You heard me, darling."

She slipped her arm across his chest, his midriff, and pressed her heated face into his neck, as if into forgetfulness, or oblivion. Robert marveled how with such seeming ease the woman could elude him even as she was pressed, naked, the full length of her lovely naked body, against him.

He had sighted Ursula at least twice before he'd been introduced to her, once at a jazz evening, very sparsely attended, at a local Hyatt Regency, another time at a large cocktail reception at Squibb headquarters, where, striking, self-composed, she'd been in the company of a Squibb executive whom Robert knew slightly, and did not like. That woman, that's the one, Robert thought, brooding, yet half seriously, for, though his appearance suggested otherwise, he had a romantic, even wayward heart; his habit of irony, and occasional sarcasm, didn't, he was certain, express *him*—as he expected women to sense, and was hurt, disappointed, and annoyed when they did not.

Eventually, they met. He was struck by her name, Ursula, an unusual name, not exotic so much as brusquely melodic, even masculine. It suited her, he thought—her large green-almond eyes, her ashy-blond-brown hair in thick wings framing her oval, fine-boned face. She had presence; she had a distinct style; not a tall woman, but, moving as she did, with a dancer's measured precision, she looked tall. Her habit of staring openly and calculatingly wasn't defiant, nor meant to be rude, but had to do, Robert eventually saw, with her interest in others, her hope of extracting information from them. She was a medical-science journalist and a writer associated, on what seemed to be a free-lance basis, with such prominent area companies as Squibb, Bell Labs, Johnson & Johnson. She said of this work-for-hire that it was "impersonal—neutral—what I do, and I usually do it well, while I'm doing it."

So Robert understood, and was touched by the thought that, like him, or like him as he'd been in his early thirties, Ursula was in readiness for her truer life to begin.

And what truer life that might be, what ideal employment of the woman's obvious intelligence, imagination, energy, and wit that might be, Robert did not know, and had too much tact to ask. Ursula was only a few years younger than he, maybe she'd catch up.

It wasn't the bedroom upstairs, which he'd rarely glimpsed by daylight, nor even the living room with its crowded bookshelves and spare furniture, but the kitchen of Ursula's rented house with which Robert was most familiar. Ursula liked preparing meals, and she liked company while she prepared them; several times they'd eaten together in the kitchen, at a mahogany dining room table, oddly incongruous in this setting, set in a rectangular alcove at the rear, in what had been a porch, now closed in, with a bay window. By day, there was a view, green, snarled, somehow foreshortened by steepness, of an untended rear yard sloping up to a weedy railroad embankment; there were tall, elegantly skeletal poplars scattered amid more common trees; there was vestigial evidence of farming, and a badly rotted tar-paper-roofed shanty that had been a chicken coop years ago. The neighborhood in which Ursula lived was semirural but the houses, one- and two-story bungalows, were owned by working-class people; Ursula liked her neighbors very much, but scarcely knew their names. She'd rented the house because it was so reasonably priced, she'd said. And because she hadn't meant to stay long—just to catch her breath, to see what was coming next.

That was five years ago. Ursula hadn't gotten around to buying curtains for the windows, nor had she taped over the name of the previous tenant, which was on her mailbox. Each spring she meant to have a plot in the backyard plowed, so that she could plant a vegetable garden; but the seasons plunged by, and she hadn't had a garden yet. Just as there'd been no specific reason for moving into the house, so there was no reason to move out.

Robert, who'd been living for the past several years in a condominium village, so-called, backing onto the New Jersey Turnpike, thought of Ursula's house, for all its air of being only temporarily inhabited, as a home. He liked it, he felt comfortable in it, he told Ursula, though he couldn't envision her remaining there forever.

Ursula's eyelids flickered, so very subtly, as if to express distaste. She said, "Forever is a long time."

Robert laughed, and said, unexpected, "Yes, but doesn't it sometimes seem to you, we've already been living forever?—but forgetting, almost at once, as we live?"

Ursula had stared at him, her eyes resembling cracked marbles, a tawny light-fractured sheen, unnervingly beautiful, as in a moment of extreme intimacy. Though she'd made no reply, Robert had sensed her surprise, her compliance; yet in that very instant, her denial.

As if, so unexpectedly, she'd been forced to reassess him.

In the kitchen, a can of cold beer in hand, Robert looked about as if curious whether things had changed in his absence. The tips of leaves on the hanging plants in the bay window were curled and browning; the soil, beneath his fingertips, was dry. On a counter, carried in from Ursula's car and set down untidily, were issues of the *New England Journal of Medicine* and *Scientific American* and several large sheets of construction paper with a child's primitive yet fussy drawings on them, in crayon. Robert glanced at the top two or three drawings, then turned quickly away.

He said to Ursula, who was at the sink, her back to him, "Why not let me take you out, Ursula?—it's been a while."

Ursula said, "God, Robert, I couldn't get into a car again

today. I was nine hours in my own."

"Nine hours! Coming from where?"

Vaguely Ursula said, "Upstate New York."

Robert said, smiling at her back, "Yes, but you like being alone, don't you. You like to drive your car, don't you, alone."

Ursula, picking up the edge in Robert's voice, did not reply.

Robert was feeling good, yes feeling very good, after love a man feels good, the burden of physicality eased for the time being; no problem to him, or to others.

He was feeling good, and he was feeling happy, as, he had to acknowledge, he hadn't felt happy, in some time.

And how close he'd come to driving away from Ursula's house—seeing the lights, the car in the drive, seeing, yes, she was back, she was home, it would be up to her to call him, since he'd called so many times in her absence.

A few years ago, he'd have driven away. Now, he was shrewd with patience.

Thinking, I can wait.

For love, for revenge?—for love, surely.

In any case Robert had risked embarrassment, he'd walked briskly up to the door and rung the doorbell, and Ursula had thrown open the door, a lack of guardedness in the gesture that would trouble him, later, when he thought of it, but she'd been happy to see him, genuinely happy, crying, "Oh God, Robert— you." And she'd stepped into his arms, and hugged him, hard. As if he'd come by her invitation. As if she hadn't disappeared for two weeks without telling him where she'd gone, or why. As if this embrace, and the feeling with which they kissed, signaled the end of a story of which, until that moment, Robert had scarcely been aware.

Ursula was breaking eggs for an omelet; her can of beer was set on a narrow counter beside the stove. Robert came to slide his arms around her, tight around her rib cage, beneath her breasts, and said, "Don't you want help with anything?" and

Ursula laughed, and said, "My mother used to say, when I was a girl, and I'd wander into the kitchen and ask, 'Do you want me to help you with anything,' that, if I meant it seriously, I wouldn't ask 'anything,' I'd be specific." She paused, methodically breaking eggs, scooping out the liquidy, spermy whites with the tip of a forefinger. Robert wasn't sure how to interpret her words.

He said, exerting a subtle pressure with his arm, feeling her rapid heartbeat, "Well, I did mean it seriously."

Ursula said, "Oh I know you did, Robert."

He said, "I'm not the kind of person to play games."

Ursula said, laughing, "Oh, I know *that*."

He'd forgotten how Ursula's laughter sometimes grated at his nerves, like sand between his teeth.

In fact, there wasn't much for him to do: he set out plates and cutlery on the table, and floral-printed paper napkins; he opened a bottle of California red wine he'd brought Ursula, upon another occasion, months before; he switched on the radio, to a station playing jazz, old-time mainstream jazz, the kind of music he'd cultivated in his thirties as a reaction against the popular rock music with which, like all of his generation, he'd grown up . . . that heavy hypnotic brain-numbing beat, narcotic as a drug in the bloodstream. While Ursula prepared the omelet, Robert rummaged through the refrigerator, and laid out butter, bread, several wedges of cheese, dill pickles. He was reminded, not unhappily, of the slapdash companionable meals he and his former wife had thrown together, those evenings they'd returned home exhausted from work.

In such cooperative domestic actions, as in action generally, Robert believed himself most himself. It was in repose, in brooding, and willful aloneness, that another less hospitable self emerged.

As she was about to sit down at the table, Ursula replaced the paper napkins with cloth napkins; napkins her mother had given her. Robert said, "A needless luxury, but very nice," and Ursula said, smiling, "That's the point of luxury, it's needless."

They ate, they were both very hungry, and grateful, it suddenly seemed, for the activity of eating; like lovemaking, it was so physical, and as necessary, momentum buoyed them forward. But Robert asked, "Your mother—where exactly does she live?" and Ursula hesitated, her look going inward, and he felt a stab of his old irritation, that, in the midst of their ease with each other, that very ease was revealed as merely surface, superficial. He added, in a tone not at all ironic, "You don't have to tell me if you'd rather not."

Ursula said, slowly, "My mother and I are estranged. I mean, we've been estranged. Much of my life."

Robert said, "That's too bad."

"Yes, it's too bad." Then, after a pause, "It was too bad."

"Things are better now?"

"Things are—" Ursula hesitated, frowning, "—better now."

Robert laid a hand over Ursula's; both to comfort her, and to still her nervous mannerism—she'd begun crumbling a piece of bread. Her hand went immediately dead. She said, with a harsh sort of flirtatiousness, *"Was* it too bad? What does 'too bad' mean? We're the people we are because we've turned out as we are; if things had been otherwise in our lives, we wouldn't be the people we are. So what kind of a judgment is that on me—'too bad'?"

Robert said, joking, but squeezing her hand rather hard, "Since you've turned out to be perfect, Ursula, obviously it's an ignorant judgment."

Ursula laughed, and withdrew her hand, and poured the remainder of the wine into their glasses. She said, "You've turned out to be perfect, too. But you know that."

Seen from an aerial perspective the desert landscape is an arid, desolate, yet extraordinarily beautiful terrain in which narrow trails lead off tentatively into the wilderness, continue for some miles, then end abruptly. Whoever travels these roads comes to a dead end and has to turn back; if he proceeds into the wilderness, he will be entering uncharted territory.

Their relationship is such a landscape, seen from above, Robert was thinking wryly. The wine had gone to his head, he was feeling close to understanding something crucial. In such a terrain you followed a trail for a while, it came to an end, you had to retreat, you tried another.

In such a way, years might pass.

Yes. Well. They were the children of their time, weren't they, this was how, as adults, they lived, so it's to be assumed that this is how they wanted to live. Isn't it?

Half past midnight, and Robert supposed he should be going home, or did Ursula expect him to stay? The matter seemed undecided. Ursula, grown quiet and preoccupied, was drinking more than usual; her face had taken on a heated, winey flush, its contours softened. Before coming downstairs she'd carelessly pulled on a cotton-knit sweater with a low neckline that stretching had loosened, and Robert could see the tops of her breasts, waxy pale, conical-shaped, with dark nipples, and he could smell that sleepy-perfumy smell lifting from her, and he was thinking, yes, why not stay, he loved her and he didn't want to leave her and it didn't matter that he was angry with her too; that (this was a truth the wine and the late hour allowed him) he'd have liked, just once, to see the woman cry.

He said, "What did you mean, before—I want you to love me so that I won't have to love you?"

Ursula smiled, and creased her forehead, and shook her head, as if she'd never heard of such a thing. "Is that a riddle?"

"*Is* it?"

"I don't remember saying it, if I did."

"You said it upstairs. You know—when I first got here."

Still, Ursula shook her head. With seeming sincerity, inno-
cence. Forcing her eyes open wide.

They'd opened another bottle of wine, a good rich dark
French wine Robert had located at the rear of Ursula's cupboard. He had not asked if this bottle too had been a gift.

Ursula rubbed the palms of her hands against her eyes and said,
with a shy dip in her voice, "I'm drunk, how can I remember
what I said." She giggled. "Or didn't say."

"Do you want me to go home? Or do you want me to stay?"

There was a brief pause. Ursula continued rubbing her eyes,
she was hiding from him that way, as a child might. Robert let
the moment pass.

He said, softly, "Tell me about your mother? And you."

Ursula said quickly, "I can't."

"Can't? Why not?"

"I *can't*."

She was trembling. Robert felt both sympathy and impatience
for her. Thinking, why didn't she trust *him*. Why, sitting close
beside him, wouldn't she look at *him*.

Robert's former wife, whom, for years, he'd loved very much,
had too often and too carelessly opened herself up to him. Like
a sea creature whose tight, clenched shell, once pried open, can
never be shut again.

He said, "That's all right, then, Ursula. Never mind."

"If I thought that it was important, that it mattered to . . . us,"
Ursula said, choosing her words with care, "I would."

"I'd better go home. Yes?"

"You'll never meet her, probably."

"Probably, no."

"My father's dead."

"I'm sorry to hear that."

"So, you won't meet *him*."

Ursula laughed, and hid her face. A crimson flush, as if she'd
been slapped, rose from her throat into her face.

Robert was stroking the inside of her arm, the faint delicate bluish tracery of veins. Her skin was heated, he could feel the pulse, he was feeling aroused, excited. Yet subtly resentful, too.

He said, a little louder than he'd intended, "So. It's late. I'd better go home and call you tomorrow."

"All right," Ursula said, then, without a pause, "—wait."

"Yes?"

"I didn't say 'love,' before. I'm sure I didn't. You must have misunderstood."

"I'm sure I did."

"I was very tired from driving. I hadn't expected you."

"I could see that."

"You don't have to call me tomorrow, if you don't want to."

When Robert, stiffening, didn't reply, Ursula said, "Unless you want to."

Robert got to his feet, draining the last of his wine as he rose. His face felt like a tomato, heated, close to bursting.

He laughed, and said, "How'm I going to tell the difference?"

Robert's present job was a good job, busy, distracting, kept his mind off himself and what he considered "negative" thoughts, the kind of job that propels you into motion and keeps you there, Monday mornings until Friday afternoons, a roller coaster. He liked even his title: Manager, Computer Disaster Division, AT&T, what a flair it had, what style, a bit of glamour. When he explained his work—his clients were primarily area banks which, when their computer equipment was down, hooked onto an emergency unit at AT&T, to continue business as best they could—he saw that people were interested, and they listened. Most of the people he met in this phase of his life were associated with businesses that used computers extensively, or worked with computers themselves, and the subject of computer disaster riveted their attention.

You lived in dread of computer disaster but you wanted it,

too. Something so very satisfying in the idea.

Ursula told Robert, medical technology has developed to such an extent, there are now entire communities of men, women, and children, electronically linked, oblivious of one another, whose lives depend upon systems continuing as programmed, without error; one day, the earth's total population might be so linked. Yet people persist in imagining they are independent and autonomous; they boast of shunning computers, despising technology. "As if," Ursula said, "there is a kind of virtue in that."

Robert said, thoughtfully, "Well. People need these stories about themselves, I guess. Believing that, when things were different, years ago, they were different. Life was different."

Ursula laughed. "It had a more human meaning."

"It had *meaning*."

"Not like now."

"God, no. Not like *now*."

And they'd laughed, as if to declare themselves otherwise.

A final number before the jazz program, the very radio station itself, signed off for the night: Art Tatum, Lionel Hampton, Buddy Rich, "Love for Sale," recorded 1955.

Robert listened reverently. He was holding Ursula's cool hand, fingers gripping fingers. Listening to such music, you felt that, at any moment, you were about to turn a corner; about to see things with absolute clarity; on the tremulous brink of changing your life.

What happens of course is that the music ends, and other sounds intervene.

Ursula said suddenly to Robert, "I saw you looking at them, before. Those drawings."

At first Robert had no idea what she meant. "Drawings?"

"These." Ursula brought the child's cartoon drawings to show him. Her hands were trembling, there was a sort of impassioned

44

dread in her voice. Guardedly, Robert said, "They're very—interesting," and Ursula laughed, embarrassed, and said, "No, they're just what they are. A young child's attempts at 'art.'"

J. LEON 92—

The sheets of construction paper, measuring about twelve inches by ten, were dog-eared and torn. There were strands of cobweb on them, dust. Robert, smiling uneasily, knew he was expected to inquire whose child it was who had done the drawings; what the child was to Ursula; no doubt they'd end up talking about the father. But he couldn't bring himself to speak.

Of course these stick figures in red crayon, these impossibly sky-skimming trees, clumsy floating clouds, reminded Robert of his own child, his son Barry, now ten years old and very distant from him; reminded him most painfully; for how could they not. He'd been drinking for hours but he was hardly anesthetized. It had been years since Barry had done such drawings, kneeling on the living room floor, and years since Robert had thought of them. (Did he have any stored away for safekeeping—mementos of his son's early childhood? He doubted it, closet space in his condominium was so limited.) Barry lived in Berkeley with Robert's ex-wife, who was now remarried, very happily she claimed; coincidentally, her husband was a computer specialist at IBM. Robert had last seen Barry at Christmas, five months ago; before that, he hadn't seen the boy since April. Nor did they speak very often on the phone—with the passage of time, as Robert figured less and less in his son's life, these conversations had become increasingly strained.

Robert was looking at the first of the child's drawings. In what was meant to be a grassy space, amid tall pencil-thin trees, a sharply steepled house in the background, there were two stick figures: a stick man, wearing trousers; a stick woman, with hair lifting in snakelike tufts, wearing a skirt. In the lower right-hand corner, as if sliding off the paper, was what appeared to be a baby, in a rectangular container that was presumably a buggy or a crib, yet, awkwardly drawn as it was, it could as easily have been a shoebox, or a mailbox, or a miniature coffin. The adult figures had round blank faces with neutral slit-mouths and O's for eyes; the baby had no face at all.

After a moment Ursula said, with the breathy embarrassed laugh, "They're mine. I mean—my own. I drew them when I was two or three years old my mother says."

Robert glanced up at Ursula, genuinely surprised. He'd expected her to say that the drawings belonged to a child of her own, unknown to Robert until now. "*You* did these—?"

"I don't remember. My mother says I did."

Robert could see now, obviously, the drawings were very old, the stiff construction paper discolored with age.

Now Ursula began explaining, speaking rapidly, in the mildly bemused yet insistent tone she used when recounting complex anecdotes that for some reason needed to be told, however disagreeable or boring. "My mother has finally sold the house, she's moving into a 'retirement' home, and I was up there helping her, she'd called me, asked me ... it's unusual for my mother to ask anything of me and I suppose I've been the kind of daughter who may have been difficult, growing up, to ask favors of. So there's been a certain distance between us, for years. And a number of misunderstandings. I won't go into details," Ursula said, quickly, as if anticipating a lack of interest on Robert's part (in fact, Robert was listening to her attentively), "—you can imagine. But now Mother is aging, and not well, and frightened of what's to come ... and I drove up to Schuylersville, where I vowed, after the last visit a few years ago, I'd never go again, and I helped her with the housecleaning, helped her pack ... and up in the attic there were trunks and boxes of things, old clothes mainly, the accumulation of decades, and when I was going through them, I came upon these drawings, and old report cards of mine, old schoolwork. I was going to throw everything away without so much as glancing at it but Mother was upset, she said, No! Wait, she'd come up into the attic with me. She hardly let me out of her sight the entire time I was in the house...this woman from whom I've been estranged for more than fifteen years. I asked her why on earth she'd kept such silly things, and she looked at me as if I'd slapped her, and said, 'But you're my only daughter, Ursula!' This is the woman, Robert, who failed to show up at my college graduation, where I'd waited and waited for her, claiming, afterward, that I hadn't invited her; this is the woman who complained bitterly to everyone who would listen that I neglected her, never called or visited, when I was in my twenties and living in New York, and, once, when I drove up to visit, having made arrangements with her, she simply wasn't home when I got there—wasn't *there*. Nor had she left any message for me." Ursula began to laugh, more harshly now. Robert could hear an undercurrent of hysteria.

"So we were looking at these drawings, this one on top first, and Mother told me approximately when I'd done it, and I said,

'My God, that long ago!—of course *I* don't remember it. I don't remember drawing at all, and I was pretty bad at it, wasn't I,' and Mother protested, 'No, you were talented for such a small child, you can see you were talented,' and I laughed and said, 'Mother, I can see I was *not* talented, here's evidence, my God.' Then I asked her what is this down in the corner"—Ursula pointed at the baby in the box—"and Mother said, 'I guess that must be your baby sister Alice, who died,' and I stared at her, I couldn't believe what she'd said. I said, 'Baby sister? Alice? What are you talking about?' and Mother said, her voice shaking, 'You had a little baby sister; she died when she was eight months old, her heart was defective,' and I just stared at her, 'A baby sister: I had a baby sister: What are you saying?' and Mother said, 'Don't you remember, you must remember, you were two years old, we never talked about it much when you were growing up but you must remember,' and she started to cry, so I had to hold her, she's frail, she's so much shorter than she used to be, I felt as if I'd been kicked in the head. I was thinking, is this possible? how can this be possible? is she losing her mind? is she lying? but would she lie about such a thing?—it was so unreal, Robert, but not as a dream is unreal, no dream of mine, it was no dream I would ever have had, I swear."

Ursula paused, and ran the back of her hand roughly across her eyes, and said, "You know, darling, I think I need a drink, something good and strong, will you join me—just one?" and she brought down a bottle of expensive scotch from the rear of the cupboard, and poured them both drinks, straight, no ice, no ceremony, in fruit-juice glasses; and she resumed her story, telling it in the same bemused ironic tone.

"So, Mother and I, we were looking through these drawings, and I asked her if that was supposed to be my baby sister Alice, there, in that box, or whatever it is, and Mother said yes she supposed so, and I said, 'And here's you, Mother, obviously, and here's Father, but where am I?'—because, in all the drawings, there is just the baby, and no other child. And Mother said in this plaintive mewing voice, defensively, as if she thought I might be blaming her, 'Well I don't know, Ursula, I just don't know where you are,' and I was laughing, God knows why I was laughing, I said, '*I* don't know where I am either, and I don't remember a thing about this.' And later, before I left, Mother showed me the dead baby's birth certificate, she'd found it in a strongbox, but she couldn't find the death certificate, and I said, 'Thank you, Mother, that isn't necessary.'" Ursula was laughing, rocking back on her heels, the glass of scotch raised to her grinning mouth. "'Thank you, Mother,' I said, 'that isn't necessary.'"

Then she put her glass down abruptly, and walked out of the kitchen.

Robert followed her into the living room, where a single lamp was burning. She was laughing softly, fists in her eyes, turned from him at the waist, or was she crying?—he went quickly to her, and put his arms around her, and comforted her, and though, initially, unthinking as if it were a child's reflex, she pushed against him, he was able to grip her tight; to prevent hysteria from taking over her; he knew the symptoms of hysteria; he was an expert.

They stood like that for a while, and Ursula wept, and tried to talk, and then Robert drew her down onto the sofa and they sat there, on the sofa, for some time in the shadowy room with the carelessly drawn venetian blinds. Robert was deeply moved but in control, he was saying, stroking the woman's hair, feeling her warm desperate breath on his face, "Ursula, darling, Ursula, no, it's all right, you're going to be all right, I'm here, aren't I? *I'm* here, aren't I? Darling?"

Doris Lessing
Voice of England, voice of Africa

Interview

by Michael Upchurch

   Doris Lessing has worn, or been assigned, any number of
labels in the course of her long
career—English writer, African
writer; social realist, sinister
fantasist; feminist, leftist, apoliti-
cal iconoclast. But few of these have
adequately described her.
  That's the way she prefers it.
  On a visit to the Northwest in
November, Lessing proved as re-
luctant as ever to identify herself
with any partisan movement or
literary theory that might constrict
her freedom of thought. Her eclectic
background explains some of her
wariness. Born in Persia in 1919,
she moved with her family to
Southern Rhodesia (now Zimba-

Doris Lessing

bwe) when she was five. After two failed marriages and a close
involvement with the Communist party in its fight against her country's
white racist regime, she moved to London in 1949. Growing disillu-
sioned with Stalinist-era Marxism, she eventually dropped out of the
Communist party and pursued interests in psychology, Sufism, and
other fields. The places of the mind and heart explored in her books have
been as various as her life would suggest.
  Lessing touched quietly, but pointedly, on a variety of topics during
a recent interview while she was in Seattle to speak at the Seattle Arts
& Lectures series. She fired salvos at such sacred cows as "political

Glimmer Train Stories, Issue 7, Summer 1993
©1993 Michael Upchurch

correctness" and Western aid to Africa. She also spoke with urgency about AIDS and the deterioration of the environment, as they affect her native Zimbabwe and the world in general.

In a more celebratory vein, she mentioned writers she admires, including Tsitsi Dangarembga of Zimbabwe, whose first novel, Nervous Conditions, Lessing is championing: "It's the first of one or two African women's novels. It's a real tour de force, that one, and she's been given absolute hell by [Zimbabwe's] male critics. They're very terrible there toward women. However, it's been good for them to be shaken up like this."

Zimbabwe is the subject of Lessing's own latest offering, African Laughter: Four Visits to Zimbabwe, which brings her, in some ways, full circle in her career. Her first book, The Grass is Singing, published in 1950, was a lucid novel about an impoverished, colonial Madame Bovary living in an atmosphere of marital isolation and racial animosity in Southern Rhodesia.

Forty-two years later—after the multiple-narrative experiments of her most famous novel, The Golden Notebook, and the controversial sci-fi fantasy of Canopus in Argos: Archives—Lessing is again writing in a cleanly lyrical vein, employing a quiet technique that puts subject matter first as she turns her attention once more to her native land. The Real Thing: Stories and Sketches, also published last year, takes a similar approach with its subtle, uncluttered glimpses of daily life in London and its environs.

A wry humor is evident in both of her latest books. The Real Thing delights in the incongruities of an increasingly multi-ethnic London: "Never has there been a sadder sartorial marriage than saris with cardigans."

African Laughter has passages that are more poignantly droll, especially in its portrait of Lessing's late brother Harry, a prickly Zimbabwean farmer who has an indelible allegiance to his race and a rough and tender love for his country. He misses no opportunity to chide his sister about her "funny ideas," then gruffly grants her permission to describe some of his: "Are you taking down things I say to use in evidence against me? I don't care provided you write down the bloody stupid things you say, too."

Incidental remarks in African Laughter make clear that Lessing is an inveterate traveler. She mentions visits to Australia, the United States and, at one point, northwest Argentina. Apart from her books about Zimbabwe, her wanderings don't turn up in her work. This seemed a good entry point for our conversation.

Interview: DORIS LESSING

UPCHURCH: *Why so much travel?*
LESSING: Well, I do a lot because I like it. In northwest Argentina, I went because I was told that it was my kind of landscape—semidesert and mountains, very high. You can go up to 17,000 feet—and that was enough. It's very beautiful. I recommend it. And the air is so clear that you can see miles of the sky at night, *garnished* compared to anywhere else in the world. So, I adored that.

And, well, I'm here! As far as I'm concerned, the northwest states are quite exotic.

Have you been here before?

Not Seattle. But I have a friend in Victoria, B.C., just up the road. She took me up Vancouver Island. I don't have to tell you of what the logging companies are cutting down. What do these people think they're doing, cutting down trees on mountains? This is absolutely criminal, just from the erosion point of view.

In reading African Laughter *I was struck by the life-or-death concerns in it that are bound almost to overwhelm a young person: degradation of environment, AIDS, a kind of disenfranchisement through lack of information or sheer inability to process that information. It seems hopeless. And yet you came of age in a time of total war which can't have been any better. Have you ever reflected whether you'd rather be twenty-three in 1942 or twenty-three in 1992?*

I never even thought about it. I think in 1942 there was a lot of optimism around in spite of everything, whereas I think people at the moment are absolutely overwhelmed by the problems because we don't know how to cope with them, really. The worst one, of course, is the degradation of the environment. You read these little items in the newspaper, sort of tossed away, that there's a good chance of another accident like Chernobyl happening. We seem to be powerless to stop that kind of thing. Maybe things will be better when you've got a younger president.

What was your reaction to Clinton winning?

I was elated. That's because all my American friends were voting for Clinton. I got terribly involved in this election. I was in New York. I suddenly found myself thinking, For God's sake, go home. You're not going to get involved in another country's election.

Before I'd read African Laughter, *I'd given thought to civil unrest in Africa, but I hadn't closely considered environmental concerns.*

Well, you see, the big question mark is the drought. That's the southern Africa drought which is a once-in-a-hundred-years drought. But a couple of good rainy seasons could put it right again. It's not the first time that this part of the world has had bad droughts. But it's done an immense amount of damage. One figure, the most horrific figure I heard, was that of eight hundred hippos down in the low veldt on the Sabi River, eight are still alive. And they've been *kept* alive. They're hosing them down and feeding them alfalfa. It's just one easily remembered statistic. If you imagine that with all the animals! The crocodiles and the pigs, they're the most vulnerable. The birds! I saw something on the morning I left—I was there just recently.

So you've been back since you wrote the book?

Yes. It could easily have been five visits, only it was too late for that. I went just to check up on my facts and things, and I watched a couple of hornbills. In the early part of the year, they eat the berries off the cypress trees because they're soft. I watched these hornbills trying to eat these berries like wooden bullets, taking them into their beaks, letting them fall, taking them, letting them fall. You know, they're desperate. And then they flap very slowly off to the woods where there are a lot of dead birds from hunger.

The other thing, of course, is the soil, which is being badly damaged by the drought. It's a frail ecosystem, not a robust one. And it's got too many people on it. When the whites went in—this is something most people don't realize—they reckon there were four hundred thousand or six hundred thousand blacks in that entire terrain. And now they think there are eleven million. And this is on this fragile land. The population started to explode as the whites came in, but nobody knows why. There are a lot of different theories. But the fact is that there are now eleven million, and most of the population of Zimbabwe are under the age of fifteen.

Now *that* is a thought to conjure with. It means that the history has disappeared from their minds, because as far as the older blacks are concerned, the Liberation War [the civil war which ended with a black nationalist victory in 1980] is the great fact. But none of the children care about that, of course, because kids don't care about the wars their parents fought. So there's a kind of gap in the cultural continuity there.

African Laughter *and* The Real Thing *use a straightforward, I-am-a-camera approach to give a lucid depiction of time and place.*

African Laughter is mostly straightforward reporting, of course, with lots of little bits from my notebook, the bits that I found amusing or interesting. I think I have a lot better chance at covering Zimbabwe than many of the people living in it because there is absolutely no contact, or hardly any, between most of the white remaining farmers and the blacks and ordinary people. They're full of the most ridiculous prejudices about each other. So that was a sad thing. And I can go at once into the university circles, and the people teaching out in the bush, and all this kind of thing. I really do cover the ground when I go out.

What was the origin of the fleeting, slice-of-life stories in The Real Thing?

I'll tell you how it happened. My old friend Bob Gottlieb [Lessing's editor at her former publisher, Knopf, who was, until last year, editor of the *New Yorker*] remarked, absolutely by chance, that the *New Yorker* had a great backlog of already-bought stories. The thing that surprised him was that there wasn't one under five or six thousand words. And he asked rhetorically, "Doesn't anyone ever write the same length as

Maupassant once used to, or O. Henry, or Chekhov?" So I wrote some very, very short stories, partly as a discipline—because you do spread yourself around.

The other motive was that people who live in London are always knocking it, saying what a ghastly place it is. I can't imagine why. It's an extremely pleasant place to live, if people actually use their eyes. That's true of every city. Why, it was just a week ago on a busy main street, I saw a person walking down the street dressed as a cockerel. Nobody took any notice! You wouldn't ever get that in a little country town or a village anywhere, because people would instantly have to know all about it.

Why was The Real Thing *retitled for its American release?*

It was called *London Observed* in London, but they thought here that people would take it as a guidebook. So they changed it to *The Real Thing*—which, of course, is also an advertisement for . . . who is it? Guinness, or something?

Coca-Cola! It's the "real thing"!

And it's also a Henry James short story. But there you are. That's what they wanted.

You've gone in so many different directions in your writing. Are there books of yours that are favorites or any you wish you could drop from the opus?

I *have* dropped one—but I'm not going to tell you which. Unkind people come up and say, "I've got that book that you tried to suppress." Because I don't think it's any good; I should have written it differently. But no, I think writers regard the whole thing as kind of a process. You try this and you try that. Sometimes you're quite surprised yourself at what you've done. I was surprised at *The Fifth Child*, which was very pleasing. It certainly came out of a very murky layer in my unconscious.

What surprised you about it?

Well, I'd been wanting to write a version of the changeling story for a long time. You know: the fairy people put one of their babies in a human cradle. I had it on my agenda to write for some time. And then I read some casual remarks by a scientist saying that it was impossible that the Neanderthals and the Cro-Magnons did not mate, and that meant that their genes must be in us. So I thought, If Neanderthals and Cro-Magnons, why not one of the little people?

Because every culture has the myth of the little people, and I personally think it's quite possible there *were* little people that vanished. There *are* little people! They're the Pygmies and they're a good yard shorter than those extremely tall people on the east coast, the ones who are doormen in New York. So I thought, Okay, we'll have a dwarf fall into a human cradle—or a goblin or something—and see what would happen.

But I had to write it twice because the first time it was much too soft. I was just chickening out. It was a horrible book.

So, even this far along, you find that you toss the whole thing out and start again?

Oh, yes. I rewrote *African Laughter* completely because I couldn't get it to gel at all.

Given the social ills that you address in your work, what do you feel is the role of the writer? I was thinking of your political activities. At one time you were—

Yes, I was! I was a Communist. That was a long time ago. Like, thirty-odd years.

Do you have any overt political affiliations like that now?

No. I'm not interested in politics. Wait, that's not true. I'm *fascinated* by politics. But I don't believe anymore in these great rhetorical causes. I'm much more interested in smaller, practical aims: things that can be done. There was a wonderful cartoon in the *Independent* [a London newspaper] when the Social Democrats were a new party. It had two farmers leaning over a gate. One says to the other, "Well, Giles, what *do* we stand for?" And the other one says, "Let me see, Bill. Yes, now, we stand for democracy, freedom, justice, equality for women, abolition of poverty..." It went on like this, right? Like the mouse's tail in *Alice*. And I think that's what I'm not interested in.

There is a line in The Golden Notebook *that says a novel should have "a quality of philosophy." That's Anna Wulf, your protagonist, speaking. But it seems very much your voice.*

No, it isn't really, you know. I can't remember the context. I do think a novel should have that quality that good novels do have that makes you think about life. Forgive me for the clichés, but it should enlarge your mind and not narrow it. If that's philosophy...

Anna also seems to have a fundamental distrust of her medium as far as what words can do. Your sheer output would seem to refute that distrust. And yet you voice her concerns, her scruples, with such urgency that I wondered where you stood on that. And if you had that distrust, how did you overcome it?

Well, I've never had a writer's block. I gave her a writer's block because I was making dramatic that concept, the situation writers find themselves in if they are political. They're always being told they're much better off putting pamphlets through doors than writing. All writers get that. That is, if you happen to be in a movement of some kind.

There is something else very basic there. There was this great explosion of the realistic novel, which does inform us and does do all these things we know a good novel does. But you sometimes ask yourself, What does it change? And that is depressing. Perhaps it changes a little bit here and there...

You grew up very much wanting to change a lot of things.

Yes. I hated what I saw around me. I was a part of this white oppressing elite. I didn't like what I saw. And I was brought up in a household that discussed politics day and night, because my parents did. So that gave me natural leaning toward politics which I have now as an—I don't know what. An attitude of the mind. I find the whole political thing one of the most astonishing theatrical performances! What a drama goes on! What about the whole business of Mrs. Thatcher's end? Could Shakespeare have done any better than that? A cliff-hanger for three days. It was wonderful. All that is very exciting. And this election of yours—there's so much hanging on it, apparently. But in the end, I'm coming more and more to the conclusion that, in fact, we—I'm talking about the human race—are always running along after events, pretending that we're controlling them, running like mad, trying to catch up with the escaping horse. Because we always come to apparently understanding a situation when it's a cliff-hanger. It's always just too late to do anything about it.

I'm very taken with some of the humor in your work.

I'm glad you said that because I think people have always chosen to overlook it. I think some of it's quite funny. That note of dry irony.

How important do you think humor is to your fiction?

Well, I don't know if it's important. I find a great deal comic, I must say. I find myself laughing during the day because I can't believe I actually heard what I have heard on the radio or something. Newspapers are really funny because they're ridiculous half the time. I'm talking about the political parts of the newspaper... the immense pomposity of them. If I actually read the gutter press, I'd find it even funnier because we have the honor of having the worst gutter press in the world.

When I was much younger, I had a friend who attended Antioch in Ohio, where they seemed to have whole Doris Lessing syllabuses at one point. And the feeling I got at the time—and it's the reason why I came to your writing late, I think—was: No men allowed.

Well, that's nothing to do with me.

But you were very much identified with feminist literature twenty years ago.

The feminists claimed me for one of theirs, which made me very angry because I don't like this separation off into sheep and goats. And I've never written specifically either for men or women. But it was interesting about *The Golden Notebook*

58   *Glimmer Train Stories*

because there was a time when I only got letters from women—violently emotional ones. But for a long time now, I've got just as many letters from men. They're interested in other things, like the politics, or things I've had to say about people being crazy, and so on. But so many things change. There was a time when, if I came to the States and talked, ninety percent of the audience would be women. That hasn't been true for a long time.

Have your books been available in Zimbabwe? Were they banned under the Smith regime? [Because of her antiracist politics, Lessing was declared a "Prohibited Immigrant" for twenty-five years under the white regime of Ian Smith, which meant she could not enter the country.]

I was never formally banned, but they couldn't get my books. They just weren't in the bookshops, or they were under the counter. I was very much a baddie, you know. Really. But now, no one can afford to buy books because of the exchange rate. The English pound to the Zimbabwe dollar is nine-to-one, which means that this book [*African Laughter*] would be nine times seventeen pounds, whatever nine times seventeen is.

I'll do some math later.

This is somebody's wage for a month. And the local books are also expensive. And the tragedy is—and I'd love you to put this in just in case someone sees it—with these ridiculous Aid people spending money on the wrong things. If somebody wanted to do Zimbabwe a good turn, they would arrange books, mobile libraries, or libraries in small towns and villages, because these people are desperate for books. And they can't get them, can't afford them; they're not there.

There's this problem with a tariff at Zimbabwean customs that you mention in African Laughter?

I myself have sent books, and other people have, too, to libraries—the Harare and Bulawayo libraries. [Harare and Bulawayo are Zimbabwe's capital and second city, respectively.] And they've asked us not to send them because they can't afford to pay the customs on them. Now, this is such a criminal business. The only thing that has changed is that the University of Zimbabwe may now get books without paying customs. But you know the University of Zimbabwe is one place, and nothing to do with the libraries.

The university isn't in a position to distribute books? You can't use it as a conduit?

No, no. Every time I come back, I get so depressed because every person I've met—every black person, every white person—is desperate for books. There are so many unemployed, they're getting an inadequate education.... It isn't like here, where nobody gives a damn about books. They're starving for books. They don't have television—or they do, but it's not very good television, not like the kind you take for granted in England, with the Open University [a BBC service that offers college-level education through a combination of correspondence courses and television lectures]. They don't have videos. Their cinema is not very good.

And I gather the radio isn't very good, either?

At the school I wrote about in *African Laughter*, the radio depended on batteries which people couldn't afford. They had no telephone. Can you believe it? Their electricity was intermittent, but they usually had oil lamps. It goes without saying there was no television or video. And inadequate textbooks. Why aren't these people with all their Aid money using some of it intelligently, and not funneling it to Harare?—because that's the way to get it all spent by crooks of one kind or another. They sit there waiting for the Aid agencies to keep them.

AIDS is running rampant in Zimbabwe. It has certainly affected my life here. I gather Europe is not in quite such bad straits—yet. Apart from the devastation of the epidemic itself, there is also this new situation where the kind of sounding of the self through sexual adventure that is described in The Golden Notebook *is accompanied by far too many threats to be quite as blithely engaged upon as it once was. Have you thought of what the repercussions of this are?*

60

You started out in Africa.
I started out in Africa, and then came back here.
Well, let's deal with Africa first. There's a big fact that nobody
realizes about AIDS in Africa: it's a heterosexual disease. Everyone assumes it's a homosexual disease. It isn't. No one's ever
given me an adequate explanation of why it should be so, but it
is. And it's rampant. Nobody knows how bad it is. In some parts
of Uganda, whole villages have been wiped out. And they think
that might happen in Zimbabwe. The difference is they've got
a very lively propaganda campaign going on [in Zimbabwe], and
there are condoms. But the men don't like to use them. And,
because of the terrible poverty, a lot of women are sleeping with
men for a bit of money. They're described as prostitutes, which
seems to me wickedly unfair because they're trying to get shoes
on their kids' feet and send them to school.

Right, so back to sexual adventure. Until they find a cure for
AIDS, that time is over, isn't it? I don't see anything else. I think
that our generation was an enormously lucky generation,
sexually, because we didn't suffer with terrible fear over getting
pregnant. People now laugh at the Dutch cap, but it worked.
And condoms, and so on. It wasn't like our grandmothers who
were tormented with terror of getting pregnant—their whole
life was ridden by it. And we went in for romantic love, and not
what one of my friends called a "horizontal handshake." But
now, you see, all that's gone. I wonder when it will come back
again. Things always go in cycles. It's bound to come back in a
different form somewhere.

In The Good Terrorist, *you describe a kind of grubby underground
communal life. What is your connection with that life now?*
It still goes on, people squatting. At one point, the London
Town Council had a policy of letting people squat provided
they paid rates [local taxes] and gas. I've always known people
who squat. My granddaughter's been squatting recently. The
same business—the relentless battle over detail with officials.

She's doing it, of course, out of curiosity. She doesn't have to.

And then the psychology: there's very little difference in the psychology of an amateur Communist group and the beginnings of a terrorist group. I didn't formulate it as clearly as that until I got letters from a lot of people who had been in terrorist groups, particularly the Red Brigade, which was interesting. And they all said, "What you have described in *The Good Terrorist* is how the Red Brigade initially started before they became well-organized murderers." And one of them used the phrase, which I've thought about ever since, "They got taken over by the language they used." If you've ever been political, whether right wing or middle or left, they use the most ghastly language. It's dead: set clichés and phrases, which have a very bad effect on the way people think.

What's the subject of your talks in Seattle and Portland?

The pressures on literature at the moment that make it all the time worse than it used to be. They range from the commercialization of the publishing houses, which I don't have to go into, to political pressures like *political correctness* and *positive discrimination*, and so forth. And then the pressures on the writer to spend more and more time promoting.

It gets very heavy as a chore: promoting. The short stories, *The Real Thing*, sold twenty thousand [in the U.S.] without my doing any promoting at all. Which is a lot for short stories. And I tried to get the publishers to see there might be a message for them somewhere in there: like you don't have to have the author out there selling. But they don't see it like that.

Is the pressure to do book-promotion tours as great in England as it is here?

Yes, very much. The thing is, I've got no solution for this situation.

You've mentioned the dangers of "political correctness." Can you tell me what you mean by that?

Well, I can oversimplify it by saying I think the whole thing is a continuation of Communist party doctrine. It's the same attitude—the need to control literature by an ideology. But the interesting thing is the people who are politically correct don't seem to recognize this. It's all the same attitude! And they haven't, as far as I can make out, taken the trouble to find out what terrible results it's had in the past, like destroying literature all over the Communist world completely, except for a few people who rebelled.

What do you suppose is the appeal of that sort of ideology? Or any sort?

I think it provides an identity for people who perhaps haven't got one. You set yourself up in it—and then you don't have to do anything else. I must tell you about another letter I got. You remember in Sri Lanka a woman, I think it was a Dutch woman, was captured by one of the political insurgent groups there. And she wrote to me: "I have been a prisoner for six weeks. And I have to tell that everything you say about these stupid people in *The Good Terrorist* is true." And that was it. I haven't heard from her again. I'd love to find out more.

Well, let us know if you do find out more—and thank you for talking with us.

MICHAEL UPCHURCH is a Seattle writer whose novels include *Air* and *The Flame Forest*.

Kiran Kaur Saini

*I have, and wanted to send, a photograph of me at age one
and a half, sitting on my father's lap and writing at a desk,
because I wanted the photo to reflect how much, and for how
long, my father has supported me in my endeavor to
associate myself with literature. But a friend remarked to
me, "I can't see you in that picture." I thought that was a
good point, so I sent this photograph in which I can be seen.*

Kiran Kaur Saini graduated from Smith College and is currently in graduate
school there. She has written poetry for twenty years, and fiction for three. "A
Girl Like Elsie" is her first published story.

Saini has spent time in many places, including England and India, but right
now she and her husband live in New York, where she supports herself by
"doing clever and efficient things with computers in corporate settings."

KIRAN KAUR SAINI
A Girl Like Elsie

I tell Mama I waitress in the Village so she don't have to cut me out of her heart. But when I come home with bruises on my wrists and she's rocking in her chair by the window in that quiet rhythm, I want to say to her, Mama, the john wrench my arms down to the floor and slap me upside the head while he's getting his money's worth tonight. But I don't say this stuff to her, because she's blind and won't be able to see in my face that I love her even though I whore. She's my mama, but she don't love no whores, 'cause twenty years ago a whore took her husband. We weren't here in New York more than three months before Daddy was shot down outside the Susan B. Anthony Boarding House for Women, standing on the street corner hollering up at some lady. She finally came down and shot him in broad daylight with everybody watching. Cops thought it was a domestic quarrel till they found out about Mama. Mama recognized the woman from walks she and Daddy took in the park and picked her out of a lineup; cops said she was a whore. I been all Mama's got left for a while; so I can't tell her what I do, 'cause she can't turn her back on the last thing. But I think she's going to know soon, since, except for the johns, I ain't bled in two months.

I come home tonight and she's sitting in that chair, looking out the window, not seeing snow, not seeing buses go by, not seeing me come up the sidewalk and cross the street to the building before I get here. She just sits there looking out, like she could see everything. Mama ain't always been blind. She started getting blind about half a year after Daddy died. At first, Mama worked at the five-and-dime. Then turned out that didn't pay for everything. So she got a job at Gimbel's, but after a while that wasn't much better. I wasn't but ten, so I couldn't do nothing to help. We stopped Daddy's subscription to the paper. Then we got the phone taken out, and Mama couldn't call down home no more. Mama started getting real tired at night and even during the day. And then she started touching things real carefully in the apartment, and she was getting blind.

When I shut the door she twists around in her chair, and once I see her face I don't want to fall on the floor crying anymore. She moves real slow now, the past couple years, and her face moves slow, too. It calms me down fast and I can almost forget about the john, the pain in my head, and the cold room I left twenty minutes ago.

Not all johns are this kind of shit. Some of them are real nice, guys you could fall in love with, if they was somebody's brother you met, or someone you saw in a park every day until you introduced yourself. There's this one guy, Marcel. He's like me, he takes care of his mother. He ain't no big risk-taker; he always want to go upstairs straight off, and not stay downstairs long enough to have a drink. Marcel don't want no one to recognize him and word get back to his mama. He don't want to have nothing to do with the bar. This ain't no real sleazy place, just dark and brown, cheap and loud. Just me and two other girls work it. Together the three of us rent a room above it with a bath so we can take up the johns who got no place to go. Marcel likes it because it's private, he can come here on his way home from the office, he says, and just relax. Only thing like a girlfriend Marcel's got is me, on account of his mama, and he gets all upset when he sees me after I've had a hard night. He gets uppity, just like we're going together, talks about killing the guy, but that don't stop him from getting in the swing of things and forgetting all about that once we're in the bed and he's really going.

I sit on the floor in front of Mama and let her rub my temples. Mama knows I always come home with a splitting headache. I smell the bleach in my hair and I know Mama does too. I put a little Clorox in the tub water and soak in it at the end of the night before I come home. Mama always thinks I been on the cleaning-up detail. She runs her fingers over my face. I don't always let her do it. She can feel a rainstorm coming in a windowsill, but so far tonight I think nothing's swelled. She says my name, Joanna, and asks me how my night was. I say, "I'm tired, Mama. You know, the customers, they're always asking for more stuff than we got. They're asking for codfish and we ain't got no codfish in the back, just fancy steak things. Getting angry when we don't got them." She understands this. In the five-and-dime Mama waited tables and the counter in the cafeteria. Mama knows about food and customers and cleaning up after other people. It's almost twenty years since she worked, but that don't stop her from remembering.

"How's Elsie?" Mama asks me. Elsie's a girl I work with. Mama loves Elsie. She knows her real well from my descriptions. Only thing she don't know about her is that she ain't a waitress. Elsie sprained her ankle about two weeks ago and was having some trouble getting around and working.

"She's getting all her charm and good temper back," I tell Mama. "She pulled in tips big tonight."

"Good ol' Elsie," says Mama, even though she's never met her. "Always bouncing back. She oughta stop strutting around on them high heels of hers."

I tell Mama Elsie bought a new pair just to celebrate not

walking with a limp. What color are they, Mama wants to know. And I tell her, "Red, Mama. Elsie's new shoes are lipstick red."

I stand up and Mama looks at me disappointed, but I'm getting more tired these days when I come home, so I don't feel like talking and I start unbuttoning my blouse. After a minute Mama turns her chair around and says, "Whatever happened to that new girl?"

I stop unbuttoning. I don't remember no new girl? "What one is that?" I say.

"The one with the big red hair," says Mama. "You know . . . Maxine."

"Oh, right," I say. "Well, she didn't last all that long. She kinda had a falling-out with one of the customers and had to quit. They asked her to leave."

"What happened?" asks Mama.

She's a whore, Mama, I want to say. She got knifed on Lenox and went back to her pimp.

"It's kind of a long story," I say, pulling off my stockings. I always wear the same thing home. A white blouse I bought at Gimbel's when they was still open, a straight black skirt that Mama used to wear when she was my age, and sheer stockings with no toes, completely nude. I say to Mama, "I'll tell you the story another time. Right now I just want to go to sleep."

I help Mama get undressed and into bed, then I wash my face and get into my own. It's quieter here than anyplace else I've been in the city. Mama hums a little bit and then I hear her breath puffing short and I know she's asleep. Every night I lay awake awhile after Mama falls off, feeling my body curve into my own bed and smelling Mama's old perfume and clean sheets.

Tonight I lay with ice on my face. It ain't every night I got to do this. Normally, some different guy gets like this every couple of weeks. But lately there's been this one. Once or twice a week for the past three or four weeks. He come across the state line for me. He pays. I don't have to go with him. I just ain't made up my mind not to yet.

He wasn't too bad tonight, like usual, just yanked me around and slapped me up a bit without looking at my face. Nothing like a couple weeks ago when he cracked my head up against the side of the car and punched my gut. I couldn't barely walk the next day, but I still didn't get the curse.

In the morning, I get Mama dressed and we go out to shop. Every Tuesday. We go to Gristede's and even though Mama only saw it for a few years, she remembers the lay of the aisles and the yellow color of the walls. I told her they painted it blue about four years ago, and she says she don't like to come so much since it's been blue because it's a sadder color. She can't see it, but she says it makes the air cooler.

Mama wants to buy apples. I know I'm going to be cutting them up for steaming. Mama used to stew apples before we came to New York. It smells the same up here as it did down home in the big house. Only I'm doing the stewing now. If we were down home in that old house, Mama'd be sitting by the stove in her chair and I'd be standing with my head in a cloud of steam over a pot. My little girl'd come in the way I used to, following her nose. I wonder if Mama ever wanted to be a grandma. She pulls a plastic bag down off the roll and starts feeling over the apples for the ripest ones.

Marcel must take his mama shopping, too. But not here, he lives up on West Fifty-second. I went up there once just to see what his street was like, whether I could tell which building was his. I didn't know what number it was, but I knew he was between Eighth and Ninth. I looked for a building that looked like Marcel'd live in it. I thought it must be the one at the far end with three stories and kind of dingy-looking windows—the sort of squat one, like Marcel. I thought about going up there, maybe, and meeting his mama. When I'd knock on the door she'd call out who was it and I'd say Marcel's gal, come to bring you some home-baked bread. Marcel wouldn't be there, but she'd open the door and I'd go right in and put my basket down on her kitchen counter (and she'd have a whole kitchen, too, not just a corner of another room). We'd sit down together in her living room and she'd show me pictures of Marcel when he was a little boy. Marcel on the bathroom floor in a diaper, Marcel in a puffy snowsuit with his arms sticking out, Marcel standing up front of the church singing his first choir solo. And Marcel's mama'd be wanting something, too, like a glass of milk or tea, and we'd shut the book and I'd get up to get it for her just like I'd do my own mama. And then Marcel'd come home, apologizing for being late. He'd have two arms full of groceries and I'd go up to him and take one from him. But he'd say, don't you dare. We can't be having the little mama carrying nothing. Now you get out of the kitchen and get off your feet. And he'd pull the bag back out of my arms.

A slew of apples thump to the floor as Mama pulls the wrong one from the bottom of the pile. I get the apples up off the floor and pile them at the back and take new ones off the front. I put the last few apples in the bag and then pick us out some peaches, too. No telling when Mama's going to crave peach preserves.

In the checkout line Mama hears the beeping of the price scanner. She says she could do this job because you don't have to read the labels, just sweep the stuff over the hole. The register girl looks at her and says, "How would you know the total?" But then she looks at me and forgets what she's talking about. I'm heavy on foundation and my face must look like a mask. I don't want no one asking about my bruises when Mama's there, but she says to me, "Goddamn, girl!" but then sees me glaring about Mama and shuts up. I seen this girl before, but she ain't seen me like this.

Mama don't say nothing, but starts rooting through her purse. That's all I need, to have to make explanations to Mama. She ain't going to understand that six nights a week at Chock Full O' Nuts don't carry the medical tab of a sixty-five-year-old woman.

It ain't like I never did nothing else. I did the waitressing and the secretarial. But these days I spend a lot more time with Mama, even if it means I got to stare down the cash register girl in the grocery store. She finally finishes ringing up our stuff and I pay and we get the hell out of there.

A couple of nights later when I start getting ready to leave for work around ten, Mama gets out of her chair and starts touching things around the stove.

"Joanna," she says, "why don't you bring Elsie home with you some time? Why don't you invite her over for dinner tonight? I'll cook you girls something real special. How about you two girls getting waited on for a change?"

I about shit, because Mama knows all about Elsie, but Elsie don't know nothing about Mama. And probably don't want to. Elsie don't believe in mamas about as much as Mama don't believe in whores. I make like I'm struggling with a sweater over my head so I don't have to talk. Finally I say, "Well, I'll ask her, but she's not too sociable, I don't think she'll come."

"Not sociable?" Mama says. "Elsie? All those wisecracks she makes at work? About the customers? All those jokes? She always sounded real sociable to me."

"Well, maybe she's not as sociable as she sounds. Anyway, her ankle's still sore. She probably don't want to come this far."

"But she's working okay, isn't she?" says Mama. "She can take the bus here. Elsie's not the kind of girl that'd let a sore ankle get in her way."

"I just don't happen to think she'll come," I say. "That's all there is to it."

"But why?" says Mama. "Didn't you say she was single? I can't picture a girl like Elsie turning down good home cooking."

"Well, I know her and you don't!" I yell at her. "So don't be telling me what she's like, for God's sake!"

Mama drops a frying pan on the floor. The guy downstairs screams, "What the hell's going on up there?" Mama leaves the pan where it fell and starts feeling her way over to her chair by the window like she suddenly don't remember how many steps it takes to get there or what's in the way.

"Look, I'm sorry, Mama," I say, going over to her and easing her into her chair. "I'm just not feeling so great right now. I'm just not doing too good."

"No, you sure ain't," she says, shaking her head. "You been uptight for weeks."

"Well, maybe I'll get a chance to call you from work," I say. "I'm going now."

I put on my coat and go.

At the bar, they've put up winter decorations. A couple cut-up snowflakes and stars pasted to the mirror behind the bar. Makes the whole place look cheerier. Elsie and Clarisse, the other girl I work with, are taking it easy and making eyes at the bartender. I go over and throw my purse on the counter and undo my coat. Elsie's telling some outrageous joke. I forget about Mama for a while.

Marcel comes in and heads straight for the bar. He's sweating and his hair is flying all over the place. Looks like he's already had a few. He slumps down near us and I say, "What's wrong, Honey?" Elsie and Clarisse slide away.

He orders a double whiskey straight up and bangs it back. I try to get him to say something, but he just keeps knocking down drinks. Then he hauls me out of the bar.

Upstairs Marcel just paces back and forth in the room. I ain't sure what he wants, so I don't draw a bath or nothing. He don't look like he needs a bath, his face is already all pink and wet. I sort of sprawl on the bed and look seductive but he ain't biting. Finally I say, "All right, what gives?"

And he says that he don't want to see me no more. That after tonight he ain't coming back and that even if he was staying in town he wouldn't never come and see me again, but anyhow he's taking off. He won't say where he's going, says he don't know and maybe don't care. I ask him if I'm included in his plans and he says I just don't get the idea. He says his mama died, only he calls her Mother, and says he's goddamn forty-nine years old.

I try to be nice about it, his mama dying, that is, but then he throws me down on the bed and fucks me almost like the guy from out of state. I try to say, Marcel, ease up, but he just backhands me across the mouth. When he's finished he leaves me lying across the bed and slams the door on his way out. It's the first time he ever left without paying when I didn't say it was okay.

In a couple minutes Clarisse comes up and says Elsie needs the room, could I get out. I pull myself together and get the rest of my clothes on. Clarisse comes in to fuss about the bed but sees me wiping the blood from the corner of my mouth with my spent pair of stockings. She gets me a fresh pair from the drawer and comes over to me, biting her lips. She don't say nothing, but puts a hand on my shoulder. I get up and go downstairs to the ladies' room in the bar. The cut is only on the inside of my cheek, it won't show. I want to wash up right away, but I got to throw up first.

When I come out of the ladies' room, Elsie's still upstairs and Clarisse has just left off flirting with some guy at the bar. She comes over to me and says she's going to take him up after Elsie gets down. That's the problem with the room. With three of us, sometimes we got to wait and maybe lose a customer. And then there's all the times we got to go out and get into a car and take a ride. Sometimes there's a room at the other end and sometimes not. Every time I get in a guy's car for the first time, I see Mama sitting at home in her chair. Mama don't go to bed until I get home. When I slam the door and the car starts to roll I think maybe this time I'm not coming back, and I see Mama sitting in her window rocking herself away waiting for me until, finally, she rocks herself to sleep.

Might be one night some rich guy comes by and I get into his car and we drive to California and live in his mansion and set Mama up in the summer cottage and hire a housekeeper to take care of the baby. Might be one night some john pulls a gun and gets trigger-happy and Mama gets a phone call about someone finding me in a gutter. Could happen either way. Tonight I ain't sure which is better.

Elsie comes downstairs just as the guy from out of state comes in the door. Elsie cuts her eyes at him and then glances over at me, which is right where he's headed. "Let's go for a drive," he says. He don't like to be nowhere where people could hear us. He don't like to be nowhere where Elsie or Clarisse can come banging on the door if he takes too long.

When we pass by Elsie she looks at me with her eyes slit. She thinks something's up, but she don't know what it is. I know she thinks I'm taking on a pimp.

I go out with him and get in his black Buick. We don't talk on the drive. He told me once his name's Barry, but he don't like it when I call him by his name. He don't want to be called nothing, and he don't call me nothing. So we just sit there and don't talk as he drives.

We drive up to Twentieth Street, and he pulls up in front of the Susan B. Anthony and shuts the engine.

"We can't go in here," I say. "It's women-only."

He don't answer, but opens the door and gets out of the car. "Stay put," he says and goes in. After a minute he comes back out with a kid in a miniskirt tripping on his heels. I think about getting out of the car right now, but he puts her in the back and we take off before I actually do anything about it. He drives up Third and starts making his way west.

He never goes to the same place twice. I just always wait to see where we're headed. We pull up outside a Parks Department garage in Central Park. It's dark and just one car goes by and don't pull in. He gets us out of the car and we walk into the woods a ways. He has me get down in the frozen leaves on my

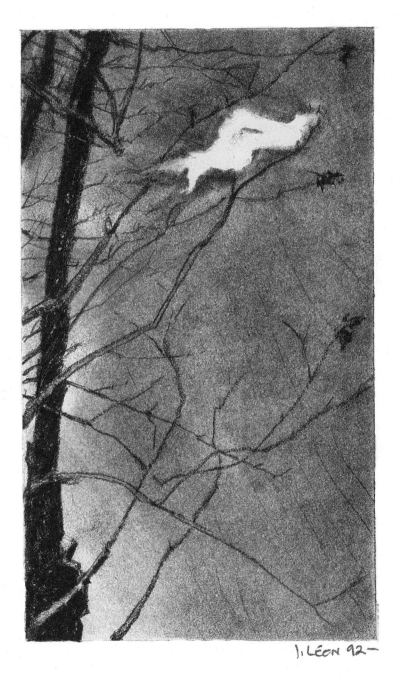

back and starts pulling on my skirt. The girl is behind him with
her hands down his pants, like she's been given instructions
beforehand. He starts grunting and his breath is all hot and wet
in my face. Then he gets into hitting me with his hands open and
then with fists. Harder than last time, harder than a couple weeks
ago. I feel his fists sinking into my chest and my gut like I'm not
even a real body. This time for sure I'm going to bleed, I'm going
to get the curse and there'll be no more worrying about babies
or getting sick in the morning. Maybe even there won't be no
more Mama, won't be no more nothing.

He's getting close now, panting and spitting in my face. Above
his head I see the tree branches crossing out the sky and then
double black comes down over me and I feel like I'm choking.
I got to get up or scream bloody murder. I throw my arms out
into him and feel my nails in the skin of his face, my thumbs in
his Adam's apple. I wind my fingers in his hair and wrench him
off of me, and the girl at the back goes rolling into the leaves. He's
swearing and trying to get onto his knees, but his pants are down
around his calves and he can't get up fast enough, and I'm
running into the woods. My heels crush down into leaves and
catch in dirt, but I just keep running with my arms up to keep
the branches off of my head.

I get to the edge of the park on Eighty-sixth. I run the two
blocks to the subway and go down. I don't know if he's chasing
or not, but I don't take no chances. I go to the end of the platform
near the stairs to the tunnel. I'd see him first from here. If I had
to, I'd just slip down...

When the train comes I get in and head downtown. It's
cold in the train, but I feel the heat from the vent behind my
calves blowing up between my thighs. Across the car there's an
old lady sitting with a big plastic bag full of cans. She's got some
paper out and she's scribbling on it with a stubbly pencil. I can't
read it; it don't even look like words, but she's writing the same
thing on the same line, over and over, darker and darker, until

her pencil scrapes through the next page and starts again.

I got to get off or transfer at some point; otherwise, I'll wind up in Brooklyn. I don't want to be at the bar if he comes back looking for me. I think about heading up to Marcel's, looking for his place again, but who knows when he'll be going back. Elsie's got an apartment, but I know she's got the keys.

I'll go home to Mama, and she'll be sitting in her chair. When I open the door she'll say, That you, Joanna? Baby, what you doing home from work so early? You get fired?

And I'll say, No, Mama, I ain't fired. And I'll tell her a big story about what happened at work tonight, how Elsie had this one customer she took a special shine to. How he was real nice to her and how she had a special deal with him. He'd come in for coffee regular three or four times a week and some of those times she'd give it to him free, and maybe a meal besides. So tonight he comes in and she wants to give him supper 'cause he looks all bent out of shape. But he's all drunk and crazy, like Elsie never seen him before, and starts acting up, pinching her behind and other stuff he never done. She brings him a whole meal anyway, because she's just that kind of girl, but he tries to put his hand up her skirt and calls her things. And Elsie, well, you know Elsie, she don't stand for no shit, so halfway through his meal she comes over to his table all prim and neat and holding a fresh hot pot of coffee and says, Would you be wanting a refill? and when he says yes, she just takes the whole pot over his lap and dumps it down his crotch. He screams at the top of his lungs and the manager comes running out and fires Elsie on the spot and I say, If she goes, I go, too! And I pull off my apron and fling it down in the puddle on the floor.

When I get home Mama ain't sitting in her chair by the window. She's up by the stove stirring a saucepan. The whole apartment smells like pot roast and baked yams. She turns around and says, "Joanna? What's wrong? Dinner ain't ready for another two hours. Where's Elsie?"

I don't move from the doorway. "Elsie ain't coming," I say.

"Not coming?" she says. Something drips off of the spoon in her hand to the floor. "Why not?"

"Mama," I say, "didn't it never occur to you that people don't eat supper at this hour?"

Mama don't say nothing, but holds her face completely still for a moment. "Did you ask her?" she says.

"We got kind of busy tonight."

"You didn't even ask her?" Mama says. "You know I was expecting her tonight, getting the whole place ready for company. You know I asked you to get her to come over. Elsie was coming. I got half a mind to send you right back out to get her."

"Mama," I say, taking half a step in from the doorway, "I ain't going to see Elsie again."

She takes a step toward me.

I see Mama come over and I'm wearing my waitress clothes again. She'll put her arms around me and pull me into the apartment saying, My poor baby, you sit down in front of me and tell me all about it. And she'll put her hands in my fresh Cloroxed hair and pull it out of my way. I'll lean my head into her and start telling her how it was tonight, about Elsie's customer and how she burned him, how I blew up, too; and she'll say how I didn't need no place like that anyhow and could get a new job in no time, and damned if she wasn't going to help me read the papers in the morning and pick out which ads I should call.

But she's still coming across the floor with her spoon out in front of her like a cane, taking a million tiny steps like it's miles to the front door. When she gets to me I'm pushing into the apartment, trying to get the door shut behind me and the wood against my back. She says, "What in tarnation!" and her hands are jabbing into me, the spoon is crushing up against my chest, gravy slopping into my bra. She's fumbling her fingers through my sex-damp clothes and dank-smelling hair, and mumbling stuff that I can't hear. I open my mouth and I'm starting my story, but I can't tell if something's coming out, because Mama don't listen, her fingers are flying over me. She's running her hands over my body like she can't believe what she feels.

Roxana Robinson

*I spent my childhood in the country. My dog was my first
companion, and later my parents allowed me to have a
stubborn, ill-trained, wild-eyed horse, whose existence
dominated my life for years. I lived in farm country, and
you were allowed to ride on anyone's property, as long as
you stayed on the edge of the field. There were no
highways. I rode all day.*

Roxana Robinson is the author of *Summer Light*, a novel; *Georgia O'Keeffe: A Life*, a biography; and *A Glimpse of Scarlet*, a collection of short stories. She writes regularly for the *New York Times Book Review* and various other publications. Her fiction has appeared in the *New Yorker*, the *Atlantic*, and the *Southern Review*. She is the recipient of an NEA grant for fiction.

Robinson lives in the country in New York State with her husband and daughter.

ROXANA ROBINSON
Sleepover

ean over," her mother said, scrubbing at the child's milky skin. Bess bent her head over the sink, stretching her leg out straight behind. She craned her head around, trying to see the back of her own knee. Bess was seven.

"Would you be able to see it yet?" she asked her mother. "Could you see the red? I think it itches."

"You probably didn't even get it," her mother said. "This is just in case."

"But I was near it," said Bess. "I saw it. I might have touched it and not remembered. I might have touched it before I saw."

"There," said her mother, and stood up. The back of Bess's knee was covered with calamine lotion, a great, chalky, pink-white island on the child's pale skin.

Bess straightened and then bent her leg, lifting her foot behind her in a slow, hypnotized gesture as she felt the tautness of the dried lotion on her skin. She looked up at her mother and smiled, her eyes focused inward, concentrating on the sensation. "It feels like a balloon when you touch it. Tight and squeaky."

Her mother screwed the top back on the calamine lotion. "I used to spend the summer covered with this stuff," she said. "I used to get poison ivy every day."

"Every day?" asked Bess, distracted from her back-of-the-knee experience. "Every single day?"

"Maybe not every day," said her mother, "but *nearly*." She turned suddenly theatrical, and her voice dropped, urgent and mysterious. She narrowed her eyes, turning her face sideways and inscrutable. "Ve-ry nearly," she whispered to Bess, the words—absurd, nonsensical—transformed, by her delivery, into code, a message about unknown danger. Bess laughed, her mouth slightly open, her eyes unguarded. She watched her mother's face as she would a movie screen: rapt, expectant, ingenuous, waiting for splendor.

The bathroom, flooded with late afternoon light, was suffused with a feeling of intimacy. Bess leaned easily against the porcelain sink with its deep blue stain. Everything in this room was familiar to her. Everything here was part of Bess's life within her family, everything proof of her mother's presence. Here was the soupy oval of soap in its dish, the soft, fraying towels, hanging neatly folded on their long wooden bars. Her father's huge terry-cloth bathrobe stretched its heavy folds on the hook behind the door; on top of it was her mother's pink cotton robe, with a white lace frill along its entire front. The pink tiles with their darkened lines of grout, the faint moldiness of the translucent shower curtain, the peeling paint on the window frame over the bathtub— everything suggested steam, warmth, privacy. Here was safety.

Bess, staring at her mother, waited for more. This was an unexpected image: her mother as a child in the long summer evenings, galloping through thickets of dense green, immersed in her own secret plans, heedless of risk. Bess hoped for more gypsy, more wildness, more of this strange vision of her mother as unreliable, irresponsible. Someone with a secret life.

Bess waited, watching the smooth oval of her mother's face, the neat rim of bangs that covered her forehead, the two thin beautiful lines that marked where her smile would be, hoping for more of this. But her mother was finished. She put the calamine bottle back on the shelf and, with a soft multiple click, closed the medicine cabinet door. She turned away, and Bess, seeing the signs, began to hop.

"It itches already," Bess warned. "I remember that Willie pushed me. He might have pushed me right in it."

"If it itches in the night, tell Daddy to put some more pink lotion on." Her mother left the bathroom, switching off the light as though Bess were not still in there. She started downstairs. Bess followed, resisting, descending sullenly, stepping stiff-legged onto each step and leaning resentfully into space until gravity forced her onto the next.

"He doesn't do it right," she called to her mother, who was now in the kitchen. Her mother didn't answer. Bess reached the bottom step and sat down on it. She fit herself into the corner, her shoulder beneath the railing, her feet side by side on the riser. She called again, louder, "Daddy doesn't do it right," and listened for her mother's answer. Bess could hear her mother's voice. She was talking on the telephone, the voice rising and falling, the tone private. Bess knew that particular voice. She hated it. Now, if Bess walked into the kitchen, her mother would turn her back—as though the person she was talking to were so important that she could not interrupt her conversation

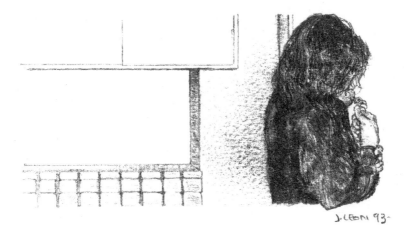

J. LEON 93-

even by the sight of her daughter. When her mother talked in this voice she laughed in her throat, playing with the long twisted cord of the telephone. Sometimes, she leaned against the wall as though she were no longer going to hold herself upright, as though she had given in to something.

"'DADDY DOESN'T DO IT RIGHT,' I SAID," Bess shouted, as loud as she could, but the private voice in the kitchen went on. Bess leaned against the wall, hooking her wrists over the railing. Once, when she answered the telephone, "Hello. Who is it, please?" she had heard a man's voice, friendly, familiar, as if he knew her. "This is a friend of your mother's," he said. "May I talk to her?" Hating the voice, Bess had given the phone to her mother, who smiled and turned her back, playing with the cord.

George, Bess's father, made dinner. George stood at the stove, his back to the children. He was tall and broad, and his body was slack, as though he were held loosely together by his clothes. He had taken off his jacket when he came home, and was cooking in his gray flannels and white shirt, his sleeves rolled up.

"Come and get it," he said to the children behind him. He began spooning things onto a plate. "Here it is, the World's Most Honored Meat Loaf."

"Meat loaf again," said Bess in a neutral voice. Behind her father's back, she made a wild face at her brother. Willie was five. He rolled his eyes back energetically, putting his hands at his throat, gagging himself. Bess laughed.

"Come on," said George, a warning note in his voice. "Children, come on." He turned and held a plate out to Bess. She did not put her hand out to take it. "Bess, that's your plate." He towered, impatient. Bess waited as long as she dared, then raised her hand to take it. The meat loaf sizzled disgustingly in its hot fat. The frozen peas would still be cold in the middle, and the frozen French fries would be mushy.

"Where's the ketchup?" she asked accusingly, and George turned and looked at her.

"Where would you imagine the ketchup was, Bess?"

Sulkily, Bess lowered her eyes. "In the fridge," she finally said.

"Right," said her father. "Here." He handed Willie his plate and they sat down at the round pine table. The room was small, and the table stood next to the window. The sky outside was dark. When their father cooked, dinner was always late. Bess began to swing her feet under the table; her father and Willie began to eat. Willie ran a small metal car back and forth over the tablecloth in a short, explosive pattern. Under his breath, he made engine noises.

"Don't," said George, without interest. Willie lowered his eyes and continued, more quietly, to roll the car up and down by the side of his plate. George looked at Bess. They had the same high forehead and straight-across eyebrows, though Bess was fairer than her father. Her hair was nearly blond, and her eyes were blue, like her mother's. Bess sat with her hands under her thighs, swinging her legs under the table.

"Bess?" said George in a warning voice.

Bess slumped heavily against the back of her chair, her spine rounded deeply as though it could never straighten again. She raised her chin and waited as long as she thought was safe. When she heard her father draw in his breath to speak again, she answered.

"What," she said.

"Is there some reason that you can't eat your dinner?"

Bess delayed again, then shook her head slowly, her fine hair swinging back and forth, making a neat triangle across each cheek in turn.

"Then would you do it?" said George. He had both hands braced against the edge of the table, as though he were ready to throw it over. He leaned forward at Bess, unfriendly. Bess didn't answer. "Would you please do it, Bess?" he said, his voice thin and knify. "Would you eat your dinner?"

Bess dropped her head suddenly, her bangs brushing the meat loaf. She began to sniff, and her shoulders rose, then fell.

"Bess," said George, "*what is it?*" His voice was not kind. He put one hand out toward her across the table. Bess sniffed again, her head still down.

"My knee hurts," she said in a trembling voice. "I have poison ivy on it." She raised her face now, her mouth drooping and shattered, her eyes wounded. There was a long pause. "Mommy put pink lotion on it," she said, her voice wavering. "But it still hurts."

George leaned back in his chair. "I'm sorry your knee hurts, Bess," he said. "You will still have to eat some dinner, however." He stared at her through his large horn-rimmed glasses. "When did she do that?" Now his voice was different, and Bess retreated.

"Who?" she asked.

"Your mother."

"Don't say it like that," said Bess.

"When did she do it?"

"Before she left," said Bess. "This afternoon."

Willie ran the car up and down beside his plate. He kept his eyes down, and made whispering sounds for the car. "Room," he whispered, "Rooom."

"Before she left," said George. He folded his arms and leaned back in the Windsor chair, its narrow spindles creaking against his weight. Behind him, on the white stove, pots stood disorderly on the burners; the oven door was still open.

Bess hunched her shoulders and pushed them against the edge of the table. "She said if it itched in the night, you would put the pink lotion on."

George laughed unhappily. "She did," he said. Bess stared at him, and he sobered. "She's right. I will."

"What if it still hurts, though?" asked Bess.

"Then I'll put even more lotion on it," said George severely.

"Your mother will be back tomorrow. You can show it to her then."

Bess swung her legs under the table. "Tomorrow, tomorrow, tomorrow," she said in an infuriating singsong.

Willie broke in before George could start. "Bess," he said in a patronizing voice, "Don't hunch."

She looked at him, furious. "*Willie,*" she said vindictively, "don't munch. Don't punch. Don't sunch. Don't lunch." She laughed in a high, annoying manner. George pushed his chair back and stood up. He did not look at the children. He picked up his plate and took it to the sink. He stood with his back to them and scraped off the leftovers into the disposal.

"Not the meat!" Bess said. He did not answer. "Not the meat, Daddy! Mommy gives that to Charleston." Charleston, the springer spaniel, had come in with the smell of dinner and was standing, polite but interested, in the doorway, his ears alert.

"Daddy," said Bess, but more cautiously.

George turned around, the rinsed plate in his hand. "What I do and what your mother does are two different things. When your mother is here, she does things her way. When she isn't, I do them my way." He stared at Bess. "Do you understand?"

"Okay," said Bess. "Okay, Daddy. *Okay.*"

George left the room and the two children sat on alone. The table now looked abandoned. The thick blue tablecloth still had crumbs on it from breakfast, and there were some dark spots on it. The children's messy plates lay in front of them, and their half-empty milk glasses. No one had told them to put their napkins in their laps. Willie, his mouth full of meat loaf, put his head down on his arm, stretched out flat on the table. Chewing steadily, he closed one eye and rolled the car up and down. "Rooom," he said quietly, "rooom."

George went into the living room. It was long and narrow, with French doors opening out onto a terrace. A big, deep sofa stood in front of the fireplace, flanked by overstuffed armchairs.

The colors were handsome and comforting: deep reds and browns. When they had first moved here, his wife had created this small world. She had had curtains made, she had covered the furniture and bought rugs. Big swatches of material had hung confusingly in layers over the arms of chairs and sofas, for months, it had seemed, before the final choices were made. His wife had seemed to have an inner vision of what she wanted, something precise, lucid, beautiful. This had seemed a wonder to George, her certainty, her care. He had felt deeply grateful, fortunate to have a wife with such power, such conviction about this place, the core of their life. He had pretended to complain to their friends about the length of time it took, the cost of it all. Really, he was using this as an excuse, to draw everyone's attention to her skill, her grace, her love for him. He was respectful and proud.

Eight years later, the arms of the chairs were thin, and faded; some had worn through entirely. There were subtle stains on the carpet, and Charleston's white hairs were everywhere, in all the folds and creases. The cleaning lady came twice a week, rolling the vacuum slackly across the carpet, but George felt, looking around the room at the wrinkled rug, the crooked lampshades, the mysterious topographical stains, as though he were on a doomed island, a tiny decaying principality that was slowly sinking, lowering itself into destruction.

He put on the padded earmuffs of his headset and chose a piece of music from his collection. This was large and entirely instrumental, mostly baroque, but with some early Renaissance. He liked music that was pure, abstract, intricate. George was a lawyer, and he liked sitting down in his chair in the evenings, leaning back and losing himself. When George put on his headphones, once the music started, he was gone: silent, invisible, passive. He could hear nothing in the old world; he was in another place. He felt he had left, that he was part of a mysterious current, this fluid, beautiful sound that swept him along and immersed him.

For the children, it was like having an effigy of their powerful father, something they could treat in ways they would never risk in his actual presence. They played games around the deaf, immobile figure, daringly shouting bad words, tiptoeing up behind him and pretending to touch him, to tickle him, to bop him on the head, then falling back, chortling. Sometimes they forgot he could see, and sometimes he startled them. Sometimes he broke unexpectedly into their games, reaching out and grabbing one of them. When this happened to Bess, she screamed with fear and joy: fear at this threat of sudden danger from her father who was the true source of her safety; joy at being so selected, kidnapped, loved.

Left in the kitchen, the two children now stared at each other. Bess's plate was untouched, and the World's Most Honored Meat Loaf had become cold. The liquid had turned into flat orange blobs, opaque, dotting the grainy gray surface.

"Now," said Willie, "he's mad. Because of you." His head was still down, pillowed on his arm in its striped jersey. His bangs fell sideways on his high forehead. He eyed her, then the small car.

"I don't care," said Bess. She picked up her milk glass fastidiously. She swallowed lengthily, each gulp audible. When she stopped drinking she gasped for breath, a white shadow left along the upper rim of her mouth.

"Why does she go away?" Willie said. One eye was closed, focusing on the car at close range.

"She has to. It's business," Bess said, officious.

"Business," said Willie. The room off the kitchen, with a computer in it and a telephone, was their mother's office. The children knew the word: consultant.

"Daddy goes to business, and he doesn't go away," said Willie.

"She only goes for one night," said Bess.

"She shouldn't," said Willie.

"She has to," said Bess firmly.

"Anyway, she went on business before and it wasn't like this," said Willie with conviction.

Bess said nothing, silenced: This was true. When her mother had first told her about these trips, one night a week, it had been different from the other times. This time, her mother had not knelt down in front of Bess to tell her, she had not put her arms around Bess and played with her hair as she talked to her. This time, she had told Bess while she was rinsing off dishes in the kitchen, not looking at her, her voice raised over the sound of the running water, loud and remote. And there were other things that were different now: The voice her mother used for those telephone calls. Their father's temper. And there were shouts, sometimes, and doors slamming, late at night.

Still, their mother left them for only one night at a time. It had happened twice. She left in the afternoon while Mrs. Garcia was still there. Mrs. Garcia stayed until George arrived. The next day, when the children came home from school, their mother was back again. The day of her return, she was affectionate, full of energy, her voice high. Dinner that night was fancy. The day she came back, she was triumphant and George was silent. He did not look at her, even when he spoke to her.

Bess pushed back her chair from the table. She left her plate and the empty milk glass. It would still be there, this abandoned meal, when their father made breakfast, but later her mother would be back. When Bess came home from school, the kitchen would be clean.

Bess went into the living room. Her father, in his deep, faded chair, did not see her. His eyes were unfocused, staring at the wall above the carved Italian chest. He was settled deep into his chair, the earphones covering his ears. His big hands lay on the torn chair arms. One of his fingers was moving, marking a rhythm that Bess could not hear. She twitched her shoulders in a rude way. George did not see her, and she put her hands on her hips and walked forward until she was directly in his line of vision.

He raised his eyes and stared at her, his eyes level with hers, and hostile. Bess arched her back insolently and stared back at him.

Looking at her father, Bess saw how ugly he was, how his hair was lessening along the top of his forehead, how stupid that looked. How mean his mouth was, how his face was full of nastiness. She thought how she hated him.

Her father was no longer looking at her. He was staring straight through her, as though Bess had become invisible. To test him, Bess slowly raised her arms, straight out, as though she were about to fly. Her father looked straight ahead, one forefinger tapping out his rhythm on the arm of the chair. Bess leaned to one side, her arms still out, but her father's eyes did not shift. He looked in a straight line. Bess opened her mouth, wider and wider. Slowly, she stuck out her tongue at her father, leering, twisting her face into a gargoyle of distaste. She focused on him hard, sending him everything she felt, rage and hatred and disgust, for the gray-brown meat loaf, the chilled peas, the abandoned house. Her eyes closed with her efforts, and she leaned forward, delivering her message to her father in ferocious mime. Her whole body was engaged, and she forgot that her father was there. When he spoke, she jumped.

"Do you think I like it?" her father said, shocking the silent room. His voice, raised above sounds only he could hear, was loud and frightening. He was nearly shouting. "Do you think it's my idea? Don't you think, if there were anything else I could do, I'd do it?" He had stopped tapping his fingers, and his hands had closed into fists. His mouth was tight at the corners, pinched, as though he were just barely holding himself away from something terrible.

Bess took a step back from him, her heart pounding. Seeing her father like this was frightening, and she did not know what to do now, where to turn. Her knee hurt, and her mother was not there.

Siobhan Dowd, program director of PEN American Center's Freedom-to-Write Committee, writes this column regularly, alerting readers to the plight of writers around the world who deserve our awareness and our writing action.

Writer Detained: Ren Wanding
by Siobhan Dowd

en Wanding was recently described as a "quirky accountant turned political scribbler" by the *London Independent*. Quirky or no, Ren was one of the first Chinese dissidents to put as much emphasis in his essays and speeches on human rights as on democracy; and at least one of his "scribblings"—an essay calling on U.S. businesses to make trade with China contingent on political reform— made it to the *New York Times*. And it is his scribbling, not his accountancy, that has led to his current imprisonment on charges of counterrevolutionary activity during the 1989 Tiananmen Square democracy movement.

Ren Wanding

Born in 1944 in Beijing, to an old established and highly

Glimmer Train Stories, Issue 7, Summer 1993
©1993 Siobhan Dowd

educated family from China's elite classes, Ren is a graduate of the Beijing Institute of Architecture and Engineering. As a Red Guard during the Cultural Revolution, he traveled the breadth of China and was sent to Vietnam and Burma. His first arrest occurred in the 1960s during an official campaign aimed at "purifying class ranks": Ren served a short prison term for his family's alleged membership in the anticommunist Guomindang and subsequently was forced to attend meetings where he received "criticism" for his opposition to the Cultural Revolution.

In 1976, Ren attended China's first independent protest march, held to lament the demise of the much-respected Premier Zhou En-lai. By then thirty-two, Ren had become an avid reader of philosophers from the Age of Enlightenment, and friends recall his predilection for debating subjects such as natural justice and the social contract. One describes him fondly as "an old-fashioned intellectual."

As the Beijing Spring movement gathered momentum, Ren posted big-character posters on the Democracy Wall at Xidan, and in one, called the "Nineteen-Point Declaration on Human Rights," he announced the founding of the China Human Rights League. The first meeting of this group, at which an editorial committee for their new bulletin was set up, took place at night at Ren's factory in a remote suburb. "We didn't dare turn on the lights," recalls one participant. "We just had candles. People crept in and didn't give their real names."

After the 1979 arrest of editor Wei Jingsheng—arguably China's most famous imprisoned writer, who is now serving the last year of a fifteen-year sentence—Ren wrote a protest letter to the national People's Congress and, just as he was pasting it up on the Democracy Wall, was himself arrested. Throughout his four-year prison term, he steadfastly refused to "repent," claiming that he was without guilt and, instead, composed a remarkable series of essays about China's predicament—on toilet paper. On his release in 1983, he found work as an accountant for a machine-installation company and lived quietly with his wife and young daughter.

However, by 1987, Ren had begun to break his silence. His "scribblings" were published in Hong Kong, Taiwan, and the U.S. His 1988 open letter to the United Nations called on the community of nations to "teach" the Chinese government about its human-rights obligations. The following is an eloquent extract from an essay he published that same year to mark the tenth anniversary of the emergence of the Beijing Spring:

> When we think back on ten years of China's social reforms, we should remember the fate of those social reformers who currently remain in prison. If there has been progress in Chinese society, if China's economy has improved dramatically, these achievements have been made at the expense of those people who have given up their freedom and happiness. If it weren't for their courage, would the Chinese people be able to enjoy freedom of speech and the modern life to the extent that they do? Can anyone say these things were granted to us gratis by our government? This decade of achievement is eloquent proof of the wisdom and effort of these social reformers, and was, indeed, born of their indignation and opposition—but, according to our rulers, their contributions to this progress are shameful and evil.

The following year, he sent another open letter, this time to President Bush on the occasion of his much-criticized trip to China that February. Soon after, the students started camping out on Tiananmen Square, and Ren, normally a retiring individual, addressed forthright speeches to them. "I have been through some very frightening experiences, but China has no democracy and no human rights," he declared. "And this fact is even more frightening." Friends recall that the students, impatient at his quiet delivery and unaware of his impeccable credentials, often hissed and booed him off the stage.

A few days after the bloody conclusion to the Tiananmen Square movement on June 4, 1990, Ren was arrested at his home. In January 1991, as the rest of the world's attention was riveted on the Persian Gulf war, Ren and other prominent pro-democracy activists were put on trial. Ren was given no defense lawyer and his trial was closed to all but the official media. His seven-year sentence and three years' deprivation of political rights was considered heavy in comparison to other convictions. His wife had to rely on the foreign media to find out what had become of her husband.

Ren is now held in solitary confinement in Beijing Prison No. 2. He is in a cell of four square meters with an insect-infested toilet. Human-rights groups have received distressing word that the sight in one of his eyes is failing fast and that he has heart problems. All appeals to the authorities for his release have, however, gone without reply.

Meanwhile, in the spring of 1992, his wife Zhang Fenging and ailing teenage daughter were evicted from their Beijing apartment by Ren's former employers (who had fired him after his arrest): Zhang returned from a trip she had made to procure medical assistance for her daughter, only to find that her front door had been nailed up. Her plight attracted so much outrage from the international community that she was eventually reassigned another home, albeit in one of Beijing's more remote and insalubrious suburbs.

Letters calling on the authorities to allow Ren, who is guilty of no internationally recognized crime, to be released and reunited with his family, can be sent to:

> His Excellency Cai Cheng Buzhang
> Minister of Justice
> Sifabu
> Xiaguangli
> Beijingshi
> PEOPLE'S REPUBLIC OF CHINA

Richard Bausch

Stories were part of the air we breathed as children. It seems inevitable to be writing them now, as if it were all a kind of training, though it was just the life we led with each other . . . as now.

Richard Bausch is the author of five novels and two story collections, including *Violence* and *The Fireman's Wife and Other Stories*. His stories have been included in such anthologies as *Prize Stories: The O. Henry Awards* and *The Best American Short Stories*, and have won the National Magazine Award in both 1988 and 1990. *Rebel Powers*, his sixth novel, was published in April 1993.

Bausch lives in Broad Run, Virginia.

RICHARD BAUSCH
The Natural Effects of Divorce

*I*n early October, Tilson's mother telephoned to say she was coming north from Miami to be with him and the baby—meaning Donny of course, though Donny was seven years old and was in fact making a show of being quite grown up about everything. Tilson felt a surge of the old annoyance with her when she persisted. He could not quite suppress it in his voice. "Do me a favor," he said, "and listen to me. You don't have to come up here."

"Honey?" she said.

"Hey," he managed. "Listen. Mom." He took a breath, and forced a softer tone, expressing concern about the trouble she would put herself to, traveling north. "And really, I'm okay," he told her.

"Well of course you're okay. It's mostly Donny I'm concerned about."

"Donny's okay, too."

"That's what he shows to you, son. Now, really. Don't be heroic." She spoke without a trace of uncertainty, in that tone which told him she meant business. "I'll just tell Herb he can do without me for a few days, and I'll head on up there. Well, in fact it's Herb's idea. So there. I'll take the train up. And speaking of trains, we'll go ride that scenic train through the mountains. The one your father and I took back when it was just the train to Cumberland."

"Mom."

"You have to think of yourself, too, Arthur. You're no good to the child if you're not yourself."

Well, of course I'm not myself, he wanted to tell her. My wife just headed out with her new love to start life all over in another state three thousand miles away, and I have a little boy who by agreement of the courts is to stay with me only during the school year and who, of course, cannot understand, any more than I can, really, why any of it, any of it at all, is happening. He said, "How are things where you are?"

"Oh, perfect," she said. "You know, couldn't be more wonderful."

He had seen her with her new husband, and had observed the casual impatience with which the man addressed her. It rankled him, as it had always rankled him when his father was alive, and he had himself been nettled by her tendency in all sorts of hard circumstances to parade a kind of forced radiance about things, as though difficulty might actually conform to one's wishes and go away if only one could have the energy to insist on it enough. If anybody had that sort of energy, Constance Wayne Tilson— now Macklin—did. In her own son's estimation of her, she was a woman who refused to look upon the facts of existence—not out of avoidance, but out of a kind of determination to be cheerful, as if to do otherwise were to be somehow indecorous.

Indeed, it seemed to him that she was quite unable to strike any modulation in the way she greeted experience. Many times in his growing up, he had observed that she was changing the visible reality to suit this trait of hers, especially where his father was concerned: the old man had been prone to prodigious rages and shows of temper, and through every tempest, every complication of that uneasy union, she had somehow managed to put the best face on—at times seeming almost blithe about it all, as though there were nothing unusual about having a big, gesticulating, wild-eyed man shouting oaths at her, and as if others, witnesses all, would believe her pleasant countenance, and decide upon the true, deep happiness of her marriage, thereby ignoring what could only have been the evidence of their own eyes.

"Honey," she said now over the hum of long distance. "Don't you want to see me?"

And he caught himself—a man standing in a kitchen with such detached thoughts about his mother. "We'd love to see you," he said a little too loudly. "Of course we would."

"I won't stay long. A week."

"Don't be silly," Tilson said, feeling heartless. "We'll probably kidnap you and keep you."

"That would be nice." Something had gone out of her voice. "A week, though. We'll see."

"Mom?" he said.

"I'll leave right away," she told him. "I've already made the reservations."

Perhaps it was not really so odd that, in the guilty moment of realizing his own neglect of her feelings, he had stumbled on the part of himself that wanted her there. And as he made plans to pick her up at the station, he caught himself basking in the practical aspects of the idea like someone walking out into warm sunlight; everything she said—including times and the names of stopovers, and what she would bring to wear—caused a little surprising stir of gratitude and anticipation in him.

He was tired of everything, worried and sick and lonely and sleepless. And, in fact, it would be good to see her.

Good, in fact, for anything to change. These days, his whole existence seemed bounded by what was unfinished, and at night he tossed and worried over what he couldn't get to—the steadily increasing accumulation of clutter in the house; dirty dishes, unwashed clothes, unpaid bills; work piling up on his desk at school. All day, each day, he was locked in a sort of automatic motion—hurrying from one frantic minute to the next, buried in responsibilities and expectations and requirements—and often by the time he picked Donny up in the afternoons, he was too tired even for talk. But Donny almost always *needed* talk: he chattered on about California—where his mother had gone—though he carefully avoided talking directly about his mother. He had been monitoring the weather in California through the television news in the evenings; he liked summer in Virginia, and he was going to miss everything. Mostly now, though, he talked about school, the foibles of his elderly teacher, the work, the frustrations and little conflicts among friends; and, even as he assumed the posture and the comportment of an older boy, sitting there in the car with him, he knew it was all childworry, all what he knew would change with time, centered as it was around a juvenile idea of popularity and what it meant, how it felt to seek it in the light of having to spend the summer thousands of miles away.

Of course he knew, too, that the boy had other worries, which he was keeping to himself. Just after the breakup and before anything had been decided about custody, Donny had taken to harboring things; he was very sad and troubled those weeks, when it was too hot to do much of anything and he'd had too much time alone, sitting in front of the little portable fan in his room, brooding about how his mother had gone off to have another baby with somebody else—someone with other children, and, as Donny put it (his small pale cheeks looking gaunt with worry), another divorced wife. Tilson and his son suffered each other's pain, really, and though they had managed to establish a routine when school started, there were zones of confusion and unhappiness which were barely hidden by the round of tasks they were called on to perform each day. Yes, it was going to be all right to have someone come in and nurse them a little.

Donny, however, disagreed.

"I'm happy with *you*," he said to his father. "I don't need to see Gammie."

"Gammie needs to see you," Tilson said.

"Is it going to be a long visit?" Donny asked in a tone of deep exhaustion.

"A week," he said. "Stop whining."

"I'm not whining."

"Look, we'll have fun. She wants to take us on that scenic train through the mountains."

"What scenic train?"

"It's an old-fashioned steam engine. We went on it once when you were smaller. You were three."

"All of us? I don't remember."

"There's a tunnel, and you weren't ready for it. And your mother held you on her lap all the way. When we went into the tunnel you said it was dark in your eyes. You've heard me tell that story, Donny."

"Gammie talks to me like I'm a baby," Donny said.

"Well, when she talks to you that way, I'll correct her, okay?" Tilson was barely able to conceal the peevishness he felt.

"I'm sorry," the boy said.

"No," said Tilson. "That's perfectly all right. That's a perfectly acceptable concern. You have every right—" He trailed off. He had heard something of his own explanations to his wife, in the days before she packed up and left. "You'll see," he told his son. "It's going to be just fine."

Was there some generalized anger in him about women, now? At work, he found himself growing impatient and sardonic with them, and their voices grated on his nerves. This morning at breakfast, he experienced a small unpleasant shock to discover a new resemblance between his son and his wife—something that he hadn't noticed before about the set of the small mouth, the cool, measuring way the boy returned his gaze—and he could not help seeing the resemblance as a defect.

"What is it," he said, leaning on the kitchen counter with his cup of coffee.

Donny was sitting in his place at the table. "Nothing."

"Don't pout," Tilson said. "You look like you're pouting."

"I'm not pouting."

"All right, tell me a story, then."

"What story."

"The story about the little boy who wasn't pouting."

"Dad."

Tilson waited for him to say more, but the boy just sat there, holding a Pop-Tart in one hand, a glass of milk in the other.

"We'll have a good time," Tilson said.

And Donny began to cry.

"Hey," he said. "Come on. Tell Dad."

The boy was concentrating on the milk. Tilson sat down next to him and waited.

"Donny."

The boy swallowed. "Nothing. I just don't like anything."

"It'll change," Tilson said. "You were doing so much better—you'll—we'll get used to it."

"I don't want anyone to come."

"Oh," he said. "That." He took his son's wrist. "I promise it'll be okay."

"Mommy's really not ever coming back here, is she?"

"Well, we know that, son—we've been through that."

The boy said nothing.

It came to Tilson that something about Constance's impending visit had caused his son to feel all the more acutely the finality of the divorce. He thought of how it would be with the boy gone through the coming summer, so far away, in the heat and differentness of Southern California.

"It's going to be okay," he said. But Donny's shrug sent a shiver of pain through him. He stood, breathed, made himself pat the boy's shoulder, then got himself busy clearing the table.

Constance arrived Friday afternoon, wearing a dark blue dress with a darker blue sash around the waist. Over this she had draped a clear, vinyl raincoat with enormous red-striped pockets; the thing was freakishly shiny in the gray light of the station. Tilson thought there was something glittering in her hair, then saw that it was sequins in the scarf she wore. She put her arms around him, and he breathed the strong fragrance of her perfume, mingled with smoke from her cigarette.

"My baby," she said, then stood back and regarded him. "You look thin."

"You do, too," he told her.

She did. The bones of her face stood out more. She smiled at him, and her dark red lipstick gleamed. Donny was standing with his small arms folded across his chest, watching everything with the wariness of someone inclined to reserve judgment.

Constance turned to the boy as though finally allowing herself the luxury. "Now, let me get my hands on this little darling," she said, reaching, with the lighted cigarette, to put her arms around him. The cigarette was filterless, and Tilson looked at the stain of her lipstick on the end of it.

Donny permitted himself to be hugged.

"Don't I get a kiss?" Constance asked.

The boy nodded, then offered his small mouth, and Constance kissed it, casually wiping the stain of her lipstick away with a napkin she'd produced from the striped pockets of the vinyl coat. "There," she said. "You've grown up since I saw you."

"Not so much," Donny said, pleasantly enough.

"Well," Constance said to them both. "I've already got reservations for the train ride." She leaned down to look into Donny's eyes. "It's an old-fashioned steam engine and it goes right through the Cumberland Gap. So pretty, this time of year, with the leaves turning. You can see for miles and miles."

Donny's smile was automatic.

"Well," Tilson said, "let's get your bags."

"I never learned how to travel light," said Constance. "I've got all these suitcases and my overnight bag. But what a nice journey I had. You know me and trains."

Tilson's father had been an airline pilot and, for the more than twenty-five years Constance and he were together, her fear of flying, her adamant refusal, even to talk about ever getting on an airplane, had been a continuing source of irritation between them. Her own father had worked as an engineer on the C&O Railroad until his retirement in 1953, and she liked telling stories about him. She would say that, because of him, she had always preferred the railroads—the lore, the sights and sounds, the extravagantly rich history—and about airplanes she freely admitted that she was something of a snob: air travel lacked the aesthetic grace of passing countryside, the sleepy rush of bells soughing off in the night as one glided through the sparse lights of a town on the plains, the steady rhythmic chatter of the rails.

J. LEON 93

She had read many books about it, and if a movie or a television show or a book had a train in it, she was interested. Indeed, she'd met her present husband, Herb, on an express to Boston, the year Tilson graduated from college. Having set out to visit him on Parents' Day that spring, she'd got into a conversation with her seatmate—Herb—who was on his way to the same small college to visit his own son. This little coincidence struck Constance like fate. She later told Tilson that she'd felt a stir under her heart almost immediately, even before Herb had done much more than say his name and the name of his son. And though Herb was plodding and careful of speech and very nervous, it wasn't long before he volunteered, with all the tentative, badly concealed distress of someone accustomed to disappointments in such casual talk, that he owned a collection of electric trains.

She was thrilled. She told him so. And later she told her son that while she was never quite as interested as Herb was in these miniature toy railroads—they were finally somewhat of an affront to the real thing—she had nevertheless cultivated a pleasure in them, for his sake. But then, of course, everything was for Herb's sake, including the move to Miami three years ago, just as her son's life, quite without his knowledge, began to unravel. The facts of the matter were that everything about Tilson's mother irritated and enraged Tilson's wife, who was never so glad to see anyone go, and who was in the process of going herself, though perhaps even she herself didn't quite know it yet.

Tilson had lain awake the night before his mother was due to arrive and wondered if some of the discomfort he had experienced concerning his own reluctance to be in Constance's company over the years had somehow been the side effect of living with a woman who felt nothing but scorn for her.

No.

He couldn't pin that on his ex-wife. He had felt this way long before her advent in his life, had felt something of it on that graduation weekend Constance had traveled to Boston to see him, and had made such a spectacle of herself, mooning over a man like Herb. Poor Herb, with his engineer's cap and his rounded features that looked always faintly silly, as if he were someone about to make a funny face—Herb had only to give that smile of particular satisfaction when his little trains were running, and all his dignity was gone. Tilson had never been able to think of the man without feeling an urge to sarcasm.

They went from the station to a steak house for dinner, then drove back to the house. Constance explained that she had made reservations long-distance for the nine o'clock run of the scenic train, and talked about what they would do up in the mountains, all the sights there were to see; her animation worked a kind of spell in Tilson's blood. A familiar turmoil. He found himself trying to interrupt her, cut her off, and when Donny rudely broke in on her to demand more ice water, he did turn from her to attend to the boy.

Later, at the house, after he had sent Donny to bed and Constance had gone to tuck him in—ignoring the boy's muttered protestations that he was quite able to do it for himself—the two adults sat in the dark of the porch, in the balmy autumn dusk, while the lights came on in the city beyond the end of the street. It had been Tilson's habit to sit out here and read, and now he felt crowded and vaguely peevish. Constance smoked and sighed and sipped iced tea; her little movements divided his attention, and of course he knew she wanted to talk. In one of the other houses across the way, someone shouted at children to be quiet. A car went by, bass notes pounding in the radio, louder than the engine. The car went on, and the quiet after it had gone seemed almost supernatural.

Constance blew smoke. "You know," she said, "I didn't even think about how maybe you wouldn't want to go on the train. I mean, I know I can be so overbearing at times. But it seemed like such a nice idea. Those beautiful mountains—this time of year."

"It's a nice idea," said Tilson, without being able to muster the necessary note of enthusiasm.

"Still," she said, "I guess I should've asked you what you thought. I'm always assuming things. Herb and his boy say—" She stopped.

Presently, he said, "What do Herb and his boy say?"

"What? Oh, that." Again, she blew smoke. "Listen, I wondered coming up here if you were—seeing anyone else now."

"Nobody special," he said.

"You haven't been out with anyone, have you?"

He hadn't. Friends had offered; he'd felt too much at loose ends, and there was Donny to think about.

"Well?" she said.

"I can't just turn around and do that."

"Nobody has to be alone."

"No," he said.

"It's not good to be alone." There was an urgency in her voice now, and he turned to look at her. She cleared her throat and then went on, "You have to get on with living, son."

"I'm doing okay," he told her.

"If you ask me, you deserved better from a wife."

He said nothing.

"I mean, depression can explain a lot of things. But not this. Not going off and leaving your husband and child—"

"Well," he murmured. He was worried about Donny hearing any of this.

"I thought you were too easy with her, though."

"Mom," he said, "somebody starts going to bed at five o'clock in the afternoon and then staying in bed—you get scared. I mean, you weren't here. It was clinical. It was real, and for a long time I was afraid she might do something to herself."

"She sure got well fast enough."

"I wish her the best," Tilson said. "The best of everything. The world on a platter, like somebody's head."

"I can't believe they let her have any part of that boy in there."

He shrugged. He had indeed argued about the custody ruling, had considered it grossly unfair that, under the circumstances, he be asked to give the child up for any amount of time; yet he had not wanted Donny subjected to more questioning from the forces of authority and justice. The boy had been injured enough by such questioning—in this, he agreed with his ex-wife: you do not ask a child to define his feelings in such a way, with such official-feeling seriousness, even if it is official, and serious.

"In my day, she would've been shunned for doing such a thing," Constance said. "It's disgraceful."

"What," he said, "falling in love?"

"She was in a *marriage.*"

"Quiet," he said.

"All right. And I know each couple's different. But it just felt like she never gave you—I don't know—she just never seemed to be quite there, for either one of you. I could have predicted that she'd run off like that. I mean, didn't you ever want to throw up your hands and just smack her one?"

He gave no answer to this.

"Well, I won't pry."

A moment later, he said, "Pretty night."

"Yes. It's still hot in Florida, you know. Well, of course you know. I was just thinking about how lonesome poor Herb will be tonight."

"He has his boy."

"You know, I don't like him much—Herb's son. There's something, I don't know, sarcastic about him. The two of them, when they're together. I wish he'd get a job and move on. I'm always like the third wheel."

This felt like an outburst to him, and he simply stared at her. But then she smoked and sighed again and lay her head back on the chair. Inside the house, Donny stirred from his bed. They heard him go into the bathroom and run water, then come out and go back into his room.

"Such a grown boy," said Constance. "I can't believe what happens to them in a year," and she began to cry.

"Mom?" he said.

"Oh, me. I'm just being sentimental. I always wanted us to be a happy family."

"We're happy," he told her, not really hearing himself.

"Look at me. Reach me my purse will you, Sugar?"

Her purse was on the coffee table in the house. He went in and picked it up, and he saw Donny standing in the hallway, a thin shadow, facing him. "Hey," he murmured.

"Hey." The boy stepped out of sight, and Tilson turned and went out onto the porch. His mother was sitting up in the chair, her hand with the cigarette in it resting on one knee. "I'm all right," she said.

He sat down and put her purse at her side in the chair. "You mustn't worry about us," Tilson said.

"I'm not." She seemed about to cry again.

"We'll get through it," he said.

She nodded, smoking. She hadn't opened the purse. The tears had left marks on her cheeks from her mascara. "I must look a mess," she said.

"You were going to tell me something about Herb." He was simply trying to make conversation now.

"I was?"

He waited.

"We always had such a lot of fun together."

"I'm glad."

"I still love your father, of course. It's different with Herb. I must say he's so much more considerate of my feelings."

"I always thought Dad treated you like hell," Tilson said. "To tell you the truth of it. I mean speaking of wondering why somebody didn't smack somebody." He now felt as if he had thrown her words back in her face, and he hadn't wanted to.

"Let's talk about something else," she said crisply. "Your father isn't here to defend himself."

He was at a loss.

"I mean I know you're unhappy, son. But that's no reason to take it out on someone who isn't even here to—"

He interrupted her. "All right. We've established that Dad isn't here to defend himself."

"He was a good father to you. And we may have had our difficulties, but it was a good marriage."

"All right," Tilson said. "And I didn't have a good *marriage*."

"Well, and that wasn't your fault."

This seemed to require no response.

"But about your father—well—I don't know what you think about me now—but it wasn't always—difficult. And I had you to think about, too, remember."

"I said 'all right.'"

"And I've been happy with Herb," she said, beginning to cry again. "It's not everyone who would tell his wife to go ahead and leave him for a few days to look after her son. At our stage in life."

"No, all right," Tilson said.

She put the cigarette out, and then lighted another. He saw that her hands shook.

"I didn't mean to upset you," he said.

"I'm not upset." She blew smoke. "I don't know what I'm saying. I don't know the truth anymore."

He watched the progress of an airplane across the sky, and thought of his father. There had been nights when he was a boy and had gazed at airplane lights trailing down from the stars, knowing his father was out there, forty thousand feet above the earth, held up by complicated processes which Tilson could not understand and was vaguely afraid of.

He remembered that he often did not want his father to come

110   *Glimmer Train Stories*

home.

"Every marriage," his mother said, sniffling, "is like a covered dish. There's no guessing what really goes on. I always thought, you know, the thing to do was to make the best of it. So that's what I tried to do."

Again, they were quiet. She finished the cigarette, then stood. "Oh, hell, I don't seem to be able to say anything right, just now. You know, straight out. Nothing comes out like the—like I mean it to. I've said things all wrong, here, Arthur, I—you see, I was wondering if I couldn't stay with you a little longer than a week."

He stood, too, now. "What is it?" he said. "Tell me."

"I—well, I've missed you. You know—"

He waited. There was more. He could see it in her face.

She sat down again, and now she had clasped her hands over her knees. "I don't know quite how to say this."

"Are you and Herb—"

She was shaking her head. "He's a nice man. He is. He does the very best with what he's given. And we were happy, too, until that boy showed up. We had such nice quiet times, you know, without any unpleasantness."

"You've left him," Tilson said.

"It's just for a time, Sugar. Until he sees, you know—sees how much he really does need me." Now she was crying again, and he took a step toward her, put one hand on her shoulder. "I just didn't have anywhere to go," she said.

"Of course," he said.

"And you were—you were going through all this, you know. I thought if maybe I could help."

"Don't," he said. "Don't worry about anything."

She opened the purse and brought out a handkerchief. She held it tight to her face for a few moments, trembling slightly. He sat down in his chair and waited.

"Are you going to stay out here?" she said, gathering herself.

"It's getting chilly."

"I'm fine," he said. "Do you want me to come inside with you?"

"That won't—that's all right."

"I'm sorry," he told her.

She had come to her feet again. "Don't brood, son. That's no good."

"I'm not brooding. Let's both not brood."

She leaned over and kissed his forehead. "Good night, my dear, handsome boy." Then she went inside.

He slept poorly. At some point during the night, he heard his son get up again, and later Constance had a small coughing fit in the hall. He saw the light, and thought to ask if she needed anything. But then he was asleep. He had a dream about his wife; it wasn't a particularly bad dream—they were in a room with others, talking, and he wanted to go and couldn't find a break in the conversation in which to let this be known—but he felt very bad after he woke and remembered it.

Later, when he made his way downstairs, he was startled to discover Donny asleep on the sofa in the living room. He took the boy's hand and said his name, and Donny sat up, trembling slightly.

"Did you have a bad dream or something?" Tilson said.

"I don't want to go," Donny told him. "I hate trains."

"Be quiet. For heaven's sake, she'll hear you."

"I don't care."

"You will care. You will learn to think of someone or something besides yourself. Please."

Donny glared at him.

"Gammie's here to stay," Tilson said.

The boy's mouth dropped open. Tilson had seen something of the same outraged look on his wife's face when he announced that he would seek full custody of their child.

112   *Glimmer Train Stories*

"Close your mouth," he said. "Stop this now."

Outside, it was cool and cloudless. The sun wasn't quite up, yet. He sat in the chair, but couldn't be still. He heard Donny moving around in the room behind him, and he began to worry that the boy might do something or say something which would be impossible to smooth over or correct; the fact was, Tilson lacked the energy for such a pass. Back inside, he found the boy sitting with his thin legs gathered under him on one end of the couch, staring into space.

"Son."

"I don't want to go anywhere," Donny said. It was as if something in his features, the texture of his skin, his solid, ruddy presence itself, irritated Tilson.

"Oh, come on, Donny. You're old enough to know better than this."

The boy said nothing.

"You're going," Tilson told him. "That's that. And if you say anything more about it you'll spend all day tomorrow in your room."

"I don't care," Donny muttered.

"This is your last warning," he said, low. "I mean it."

His mother was coming down the stairs. They watched her bone-thin legs, saw the bright red skirt she wore, the shiny black belt. Constance put one hand on the railing and leaned down to look at them. "Am I interrupting anything?"

"Good morning," Tilson said.

She came into the room and stood before them in the skirt. Her blouse was a bright shade of pink. There were frills down the front of it. "What do you think? Be honest."

"Very nice," Tilson said. It seemed to him that these were the clothes of a much younger woman; the skirt came to well above the knees, and the frills of the blouse had a feathery sort of softness that made her look vaguely puffy, almost pigeon-chested. He kept the smile on his face, and Donny shifted on the couch, suddenly interested in something between the toes of his left foot.

"Donny, what do you think, Sugar."

"Nice," he said, without looking up.

"Well," said Constance, turning her attention to the weather outside the open door. She stood at the screen and breathed. "A beautiful, beautiful fall day."

"It's a little nippy," Tilson said. "We'll need to wear jackets."

"Let's eat at that diner on the way," said his mother.

"I'm not hungry," Donny said.

"The mountain air will make you hungry."

"I don't think so."

"Well," said Tilson with a definiteness he meant for his son to understand, "you'll see."

The boy said little as they prepared for the trip, but he went along with it all. In fact, he went out and sat in the car to wait for them, his jacket wrapped around his middle, his hands folded in his lap. Tilson followed Constance down the walk to the car, and her heels clattered on the pavement, a cheery, busy sort of sound. There was a jauntiness to her step which for some reason made him feel an obscure sense of pity for her, as though someone had already said something withering or sardonic. He opened the passenger door of the car and she got in, arranging herself, turning to give Donny a smile. "So handsome, sitting there," she said.

"Thank you," said Donny, with a faint supercilious nod of his head.

"I think he's a sourpuss," Tilson said, and gave his son a warning look. Without waiting for a reaction, he closed the door and walked around the back of the car, seeing their shadow-shapes in the rear window and thinking of them waiting in silence for him. His mother had pulled the rearview mirror around to check the line of her lipstick. She adjusted it as he got in, but it was crooked, showing him not the road behind them but Donny's pouting face. The boy was staring glumly out the window. Tilson readjusted the mirror, then started the car.

"Ah," his mother said. "I love to be heading out on a trip. Let's see if we can hold off breakfast until the train gets up to its turn-around point. We can eat there, up in the mountains."

"That'll be close to eleven won't it? I know Donny says he's not hungry, but I think he should eat something before then."

"I already had a bowl of cereal," Donny said. "Before anybody got up."

"You see?" said Constance. "And you and I can hold out."

Tilson looked back at this son. "Thanks, pal. That does make it easier."

"Don't call me 'pal,'" he muttered.

Tilson chose to ignore this, and they all rode on in silence for a time.

"Gammie, how come you're staying with us?" Donny said.

Constance took a moment to answer. "It's just until Herb's boy can find a job. It's a bit crowded, you know."

"I know," Donny said pointedly.

"Hey, boy," said Tilson, "you watch your tone."

His mother looked at him, but said nothing.

They crossed into Maryland, still heading north and west. The road wound upward, into the mountains, around bluffs of rock, through the shade of overhanging oaks and sycamores. Along a wide crown of grass and flowers, they passed a sign advertising the scenic train. Constance turned in the seat to address her grandson. "This train goes on a real track seventeen miles right up through the Cumberland Gap."

Tilson now wished he could see Donny's face in the rearview mirror; the boy's silence was awkward. "Son?"

"He's enjoying the scenery out the window," Constance said.

"Donny."

"What."

"Did you hear what Gammie said to you?"

"I was watching the trees," Donny said, with an edge of petulance.

"They get occupied," said Constance. "You used to daydream like that, and no one could get through to you."

He remembered once pretending to concentrate on the dull text of a history book rather than responding to her forced cheerfulness. When had that been? His father was still alive. A long drive to New York for some business with the Airline Pilots Association. His father had been unscrolling, mile upon mile, the epic proportions of his unhappiness, sniping at her, being scornful and caustic, and Tilson could not stand that she took it from him. He had seen the white oval of her face turned to him, heard the small vivacious insistence of her voice, the straining for brightness, and a part of him had hated her for it.

Recalling this now, something moved just under his heart. "Donny," he said. "Gammie spoke to you."

"Don't," Constance said. "Really."

"I'm not going to tolerate it," Tilson told his mother. "Unhappiness is not an excuse for rudeness, Donny."

"*Okay,*" Donny said.

"Apologize this instant."

"I'm sorry," the boy muttered.

They were quiet again. The road curved and climbed through the mountains, and out into a clear vision of Cumberland with its white houses scattered in the dips and hollows of the steep hills and its square-roofed, sign-painted dark brick buildings ranked across from each other on the Main Street. The old train depot was beyond an abandoned foundry and parking lot, and a crowd was already gathering there.

"Good thing we left when we did," Constance said, her voice trembling only a little. She smiled slightly, glancing back at her grandson, then opened her purse and peered into it, for her cigarettes, no doubt—though now her bony features betrayed her, becoming faintly mournful, the watery, light blue eyes frowning with concentration, looking almost panic-stricken—and Tilson had a moment of feeling what it must be to have her troubles, to have been through everything she had been through. For that instant he was weirdly separate from her, felt the arc of her life as if it were the life of a stranger, and it made him wince inwardly. He watched, almost awestruck, while she began picking through the contents of the purse, as though somewhere at the bottom of it might be the one answer, the one something which would stop the progress of her bewilderment and her pain, and let her rest at last, relax at long last, those nerves with which she had, all the years, kept her brave smile turned upon the world.

"What an ugly building," Donny said.

Tilson reached back and took his son by the wrist. "Don't make up your mind before you know what you see," he said. "You're not old enough to know." He'd held the small wrist too tightly, and the boy began to cry.

"Arthur, for heaven's sake," his mother said, hurrying out of the car, throwing her purse over her shoulder and opening the back door. "Come here, Sugar."

Donny scooted across the seat and into his grandmother's arms. "There," Constance said. "It most certainly is an ugly building." They walked off together across the parking lot.

Abandoned by them, Tilson locked the car, then followed, remaining a few steps behind. There was still the rest of the day to do, the rest of whatever the next few weeks would be, and he felt it all like a weight on his heart. He had not meant to cause any ill-feeling or upset; he had merely wanted his son to understand how wrong about simple things a person could be.

Off in the distance, the train whistle sounded, exactly as he remembered it. The wind blew. Leaves rattled in the sunlit corners of the lot. A few feet away, his pouting son turned slightly and gazed at him. Tilson forced a smile.

Stewart David Ikeda

*Just days before my birthday, it was the end of the sixties,
my terrible twos, and my perpetual summer of love. "Hey
Jude" pumped constantly from every jukebox that summer;
I was young and restless, and hit the road, just me, Mom,
and our Harley moped!*

Stewart David Ikeda, twenty-six, is a free-lance writer and editor of several
publications at the University of Michigan, Ann Arbor, where he taught
creative writing and where he earned an M.F.A. on a Rackham Merit
Fellowship and two Avery & Jule Hopwood awards for a novel-in-progress
and a story collection. His poetry and prose have appeared in *Ploughshares* and
NYU's *Minetta Review,* among other publications, and have received awards
from NYU, the *Kentucky State Poetry Society,* and *A Different Drummer*
magazine.

Ikeda, raised in Philadelphia, now lives in Ann Arbor, Michigan.

STEWART DAVID IKEDA
Roughie

*I*t's a TV voice replaying in your mind, saying a life don't matter, as you watch Little Man hiding from a service revolver. And what's one more or less dog's life anyway?

Little Man bent over behind a reeking Dumpster, crying. Just home from school—still wearing his knapsack, his Turtles bag, still holding the clay candlestick he made in pottery—to find his father in the pen out back with Roughie, pistol in one hand, other trying to lock the gate behind with an old, tied-up electric cord. And Little Man's stepsisters crying too, faces pressed up against the storm fence like at the zoo.

Sound of backfire on the street. His father usually says, That's just a car backfiring, Little Man. Maybe firecrackers. Just take the girls down in the basement and finish your homework. But now, Little Man hears the boom and jumps anyway.

Get back! his father tells the girls, in his big bullhorn cop's voice. GET BACK NOW!

They just go on. He slaps the fence, knocks them on their butts. Tama staying down, holding her head, but crying on and on, not missing a beat. Singing out, Don't do it, don't do it— and Maddy as usual saying nothing.

Little Man collects himself, breathing trash, old chicken from the Dumpster, mourning Roughie. 'Til he can't stand it. 'Til best thing's to get it done, fast, clean, over and out. Makes him leave his cave to watch, maybe help—but swearing aloud he won't shoot her himself.

Roughie looking electrocuted, shaking like an old dying woman. Growling, like she knows a magnum got a bead on her. Glazey-eyed, drooling like Little Man seen on that old junkie booting on the stoop yesterday. Only, old junkie felt no pain. Roughie, she'd beg for it herself if she could speak. She'd be brave, say, Right between the eyes, and hold her breath to make an easier target. But here she's not in her right mind, hurting with rat fever.

Do it, Daddy, Little Man says, hopping the fence. He's a rare boy that way—so sharp and stubborn—just views a situation and, right off, knows what time it is, makes the decision, sticks to it like Krazy Glue. 'S why he's in that school gifted program— got that hardheaded sticking power, like now, with his little heart breaking, he sticks solid with his father. Says, I'll get the gate—she won't get out. Make the pain stop, Daddy.

Little Man's father eyeballs the boy. Red-eyed, clear as day he's been chugging a few hard ones. Feeling painless himself, or anyway won't remember it. Stink-breath and wobbly, his gun hand waves up and down in slo-mo like a palm tree on "Hawaii Five-O." Tells Little Man, Fuck off outta here now, boy. Take your sisters in the house.

I gotta stay with Roughie. She'll be scared if I ain't with her.

When his father whops him, Little Man's nose starts spilling over his white shirt, but he don't back off one milli-inch. Just standing, not even crying. In this miserable, man-sized voice too big for his small body, he says, You heard Daddy, you girls get in the house now, quick. Roughie won't stop hurting 'til you go. Please.

Like she's been possessed all sudden, Tama stops bawling, blinks her big eyes, and gets up off the ground, still holding her head. Maddy follows—scared to be two feet away from Tama.

Door slams behind, and you hear Tama shout inside, He ain't *our* daddy. And Little Man's father, dark as a storm, shout, You just wait, you little bitch! You're in my goddammed house now!

But Little Man digs in next to his father and waits, just waiting like Buddha. Soft as a park pigeon, he says, Roughie—Daddy, please.

His father looks at the gun stupidly, then raises it at Roughie, zombielike, like since he don't know what to do he decides better just shoot something. But then, Daddy's all shaky, got the quivers, and there's a click, then a pop, just like that. Flame from around the barrel, just like when you first stick a match in the oven pilot that's been off for a while. Shot's not so loud itself, but keeps going and going on, bouncing like a Super Ball up and down the backs of the yards and houses.

You wait for it to stop and all to quiet down, but then hear a terrible, terrible whine, like a sick baby crying at night, but it's Roughie. See her caved down in front, ass hung high in the air, shivering like she's in Alaska without an igloo. The most beautiful dog ever. Makes you wanna cry yourself, seeing her chest, all sexy and hairy white and gold, with a big red chunk out of it, and she down begging on her front paws with the side of her face and nose in the dirt. That son of a bitch ... old, drunk, shaky son of a bitch missed from no feet, only took a fat piece outta her heart, but didn't finish the job. You wonder how this sorry shot, always strutting around big Mister John Wayne policeman, ever killed a man before.

Little Man and his father froze stiff, locked up, like before they wasn't scared of no rabid dog, but a half-dead, miserable pile of bloody hair scared them into mummies. Hear Tama just inside the screen door, wailing louder than ever. Look around and notice heads popping out of neighbors' houses, the two Johnson boys opening and closing the blinds at their rear window, ducking back. See that giant, Octavius, bolt out into his yard, shirtless, rippling like Arnold Schwarzenegger, carrying his own piece and looking dizzy and blinded like he just woke up.

Oh shit, shit, he shot her. Devil shot Roughie. Po-lice bru-tal-i-ty!

Everybody buzzing and hushing each other and clucking their tongues, even weeping, because near everyone loved Roughie. They knew her, remember her hounding the grocer, stalking the subway, trucking after the Good Humor van, summertime, playing with kids in the sprinkler. Lotta folks think more of her than Little Man's father. Now he's scanning around looking trapped, shouting, Mind your own nosy businesses; there's nothing for you to see here. He starts swinging 'round with the pistol, pointed down a little, and you see the heads pop back into their houses like squirrels in a tree, except for Octavius. He just spits and yells, Yessir, Officer, and starts back in, slow. But even Octavius loved that Roughie. Yells, She worth twenty of you, before disappearing.

Roughie's ass comes down, finally, crumples over into the dirt

in a heap. If anything on this earth worse than readying yourself to die, then getting only *half* killed, only Jesus can tell you what that is.

Little Man's the first one of them to snap to. All four foot something of him jerks awake, and with those tiny brown hands he tries to take the pistol from his daddy. That wakes up Senior. Says, Get back, damn you; you'll get hurt, don't ...

And Little Man: We can't leave her like that, Daddy. It's okay, I'll do it, I know you don't want to do it. I can do it.

See, a special boy—Little Man's no coward. He adjusts. He floats.

There's a blur and scuffle, and old Roughie lifts up her eyes like she'll pull the trigger herself with just willpower, then POP! and this time you wait for the bouncing to stop. Pop, pop, down the block, and it's all quiet and you hold your breath and pray for Roughie. 'Til she starts whimpering again.

Then you see Little Man. His expression all squirming brown pain; looking old, used, in his white button shirt and leather belt that wraps near twice around his skinny body, *strangling* that pistol. Got that bulging knapsack, half as big as he is, piled on him, like a midget soldier in a Vietnam movie. And camouflage eyes to match—frosty, into the North Pole, gone. You see his fingers start squeezing again.

It's the voice in your mind and on the TV that says a life don't matter. But a life's not nothin'. You're pissed. But you're outta there, fast as feet will take you. And you don't know how things ended up for Roughie.

Katherine Min

*1965. It is my first trip to Korea. I am six. Here I am with
my mother and father, my father's parents, and my cousins.
I am wondering why no one speaks English.*

Katherine Min was a 1992 recipient of a National Endowment for the Arts grant for fiction writing. Her work has appeared in *Ploughshares, Special Report: Fiction, Beloit Fiction Journal,* and other magazines, and is forthcoming in *Triquarterly* and *Confrontation.* One of her stories was anthologized in *Worlds of Fiction,* published by Macmillan last fall. She has recently completed a novel, *Stealing the View.*

Min lives in Plymouth, New Hampshire, with her husband and two children.

KATHERINE MIN
Objects

I've become an heir to hangers. They are abundant in my mother's house, made of blue plastic and thin wire, with crisp paper linings and without; wooden presses for slacks; tiered clip-ons for skirts; the kind with hooks on either side for spaghetti-strap dresses. My mother used to hang up every-thing—T-shirts, socks, even underwear—starching them first and ironing them in severe creases, until the clothes did not so much hang as perch, like small clawed birds.

Now empty hangers clatter sadly inside empty closets. The clothes that once hung here, that each hanger represents, I have packed carefully away in boxes marked SALVATION ARMY and SAVE FOR JILL. A few I have stuffed in my own canvas bag. Alone in the house, I am uneasy. My mother has been dead for two weeks and there is a settling of dust that would not have stood a chance during her administration. I feel its presence like the violation of some cease-fire agreement. The displacement of dust seemed my mother's mission; this house, repository of dirt, was my mother's house. It occurs to me in a morbid way that my mother is now becoming what she fought so hard in life to vanquish. Ashes to ashes. Duster to dust.

"Life is maintenance," my mother was fond of saying, as she skidded the vacuum cleaner across the living room carpet, or scoured the kitchen counters with a scrub brush and bleach. It was part of the immigrant work ethic, I thought. She'd left Korea after the war, arriving at Pine Manor Junior College with fifty dollars and a steamer trunk of drab Western clothes, heavy sweater and skirt sets that made her look, in the old photographs, like a standing column of laundry. She was full of hardship stories of living in basements, subsisting on insect-infested grain and watery cabbage soup, sewing skirts from woven rice sacks. My mother hoarded rubber bands and pieces of string, reused plastic bags until they grew wrinkled and soft, and bought huge quantities of canned food, anticipating some dire shortage. And in the meantime, she swept and dusted and washed and ironed, as though, in return for her release from wartime basements, she had pledged an oath of domestic servitude.

Because my mother was fanatical about housecleaning did not mean she possessed a natural aptitude. In fact, she was clumsy. She washed dishes fast and hard, with plenty of soap suds and steaming water, but she often broke a glass in the strainer, trying to pile the dishes too high. Scrubbing with steel wool between the fork tines, she would get it stuck and pull in frustration until the thing unraveled. She was impatient with my efforts to help her, preferring to "just get it done," and so I grew up spoiled, lying reading on the couch while she moved around me like a tropical storm.

When someone close to you dies, they seem to go out of focus; you forget the most familiar things, details of their voice and gestures. It is a kind of shock, I think—death, awesome, irrevocable, momentarily becoming the only fact about the person, the only thing known.

So I take up objects, to re-create her, start with the tangible things left behind. In my mother's bedroom closet, I find a set of three Samsonite suitcases in white textured plastic. They look new. Their chrome fixtures are shiny as mirrors, surfaces unscuffed and perfectly molded. As far as I know, they have never been used.

It did not seem strange to me at the time that my mother should want so badly, and with such vengeance, this set of matching luggage. I was eight or nine then and I had seen her steamer trunk in the storage basement, that monstrous black box in which my mother had freighted her hopes to a new world. The Samsonite suitcases would not have supported the heavy woolen wardrobe of my mother's past; they were too sleek, too American. They would be filled with synthetic fabrics, light silken things in whites and beiges.

My father, who was a quiet man with a distracted mind and a tolerance for my mother's whims, wanted a lawn mower instead. "What do we need luggage for?" I remember him asking. As protest goes, it was a flea slap.

But my mother would not offer explanations. She rested her finger in the pages of her magazine—*Vogue* or *Glamour*. "Oh, Jae Myung," she said, lightly. "It's all right."

It was my job to stick the S & H green stamps into the books. I sat at the kitchen table. My legs were not long enough to reach the floor; I wrapped and unwrapped them around the cold metal chair legs, kicking them easily through the air. I took the stamps out of the wrinkled envelope in which they were kept and pressed them against the sponge which my mother had moistened and laid out on a saucer. Positioning them carefully on the newsprint pages, within the prescribed outlines, I pushed down with the heel of my hand.

My mother leaned over me, her forearms flat against the table. "How's it coming?" she asked. She watched as I stuck the last of the stamps in. Then she counted the books, sliding into the chair as I slid out. Her mouth moved in mute calculation, flicking the books upward with her fingers, one by one, until she reached the end of the pile.

"Good job, Eleanor," she said, rubbing the top of my head. "Twelve more, and we're done."

When the stamps were redeemed, my mother set the luggage in the center of the living room carpet, like sculpture. She arranged the suitcases parallel to one another, evenly spaced, and beamed at them, touched them as if in disbelief, rubbed a thumb over their chrome locking mechanisms.

I see her now, the way she was then, her black hair succumbing slowly to silver, nose embedded with dark ovals on either side where her glasses sit. Her face is heart-shaped, with broad, smooth cheeks that always felt slightly slick. She is beautiful. This is what I remember suddenly. An important detail.

Spread out across my mother's dressing table are bottles half filled with goo of varying consistencies. There are facial softeners, astringents, eye wrinkle and throat creams, skin cleansers, moisturizing lotions, and all-night beauty treatments. Also, there are tubes of lipstick in pale pinks and dark reds, little pots of blush and eye shadow, and pencil sticks of eyeliner with blunt blue ends. I try them all—making my face up in high gloss and shades of reds and purples—and stare at myself in the mirror. It is not my mother's face.

I remember the way my father would look at her when she wore her red dress with the black shapes like shadows, her hair swept up from a face that reflected light, that shone, swathed in colors like a painting. His thin, angled face turned solemn, as though in the presence of miracles.

My mother's absence makes me hungry for details. I am ashamed by my curiosity. There is no excuse for what I am doing here, left alone amid my mother's things. There is a locked drawer in my mother's desk in the study. I don't remember it from my childhood. I find a small key under the embroidered cloth that lies on the dressing table. It fits the lock, and that is how I find them, the vertical stack of letters in pale blue envelopes enclosed by a rubber band, all of them written by one person—Daniel Rollins—a name I do not remember ever hearing in my life.

I feel myself go wary, my hands around the letters infirm. It's almost as though I had known they would be here. I start reading the letters at random, replacing each one in its envelope with absurd care, as though she might catch me still.

"You are the most exciting woman I've ever met, Kyoung Ja," he writes in a large, straight hand. "My love for you is as boundless as it is impossible. I am certain it will go on for as long as I live."

Daniel Rollins's letters are filled with lyric poetry, with extravagant reflections on love and destiny—all the touching, banal phrases. I am embarrassed reading them; that they are addressed to my mother seems more unlikely than shocking. She may have been beautiful, but she was still my mother. And it is clear from his words that she wrote letters of her own.

"Kyoung Ja, you brought back some wonderful memories! I'll never forget that day either, the way the sunlight shone like a halo around your hair and seemed to radiate from your eyes. You were wearing that white lace dress and silver jewelry that made music when you moved. I couldn't pay attention to a word poor Jae was saying. I was completely taken. I wanted everyone to go away and leave us alone."

I want to read them all, but there are so many. My eyes begin to burn, to ache. I scan postmarks, '66, '67, on to '76. A decade of letters. In the last one, he writes: "Despite everything, Kyoung Ja, I know I will always love you deeply, more than I have ever loved or will ever love anyone. I can't turn off my emotions like a water faucet, though you may be able to. Jae is a good man, it's true, but you will never feel for him what we have felt for each other. You've said it yourself. You have had many unhappy years, Kyoung Ja, and now for the rest of your life there will be a gap where our love has been, a loneliness."

I put the letters down. This last was written a year before my father's death.

I was twelve years old, lying in the dark late at night. The sheets were hot and crumpled, binding me too tightly around the legs. I threw them off. My ears strained for the sound of voices, my parents speaking in low, urgent tones, in the language they used together when they did not want me to understand. I listened with apprehension, not for the first time, trying to imagine what it was they were speaking of so violently in the middle of the night, what decisions they were coming to that might affect my life.

I got out of bed and tiptoed to the door of my parents' bedroom. They had stopped talking and a strange sound came from inside. My father was crying, sobbing in long, uncontrolled spasms. I could hear my mother's low whisper.

The next morning, my father had already left for work. My mother sat at the kitchen table in her robe, her hair wrapped in a towel. She looked cold and clean, remote. I asked about what I'd heard and she stopped a moment before setting her coffee cup down.

"Oh, Eleanor," she said. "It was just a misunderstanding. It's fine now." She shrugged. "Sorry we disturbed you."

My father was dead a year later. A brain tumor squeezed from him first thought, then life, which, for my father, was like dying twice. Cast from the intellectual realm, he grew sullen and tiny. Toward the end, my mother could pick him up from the bed to change his bed sheets, could carry him to a chair like an oversize cloth doll. He clutched her arms and whispered to her in Korean, urgently, unintelligibly. The last clear thing he said to me before he died was, "I love your mother more than my life."

I call information and get the number for a Daniel T. Rollins in Nashua, New Hampshire. I try to picture him, his broad Caucasian features with long, sleepy eyelashes and startling blue eyes. I think of the day I told my mother I was going to marry Jack. She nodded, her lips puckered in approval. "American man, that's good," she said. "Share housework."

In the sixteen years since my father's death, she had never mentioned another man. If I suggested she go out with some widower or aging bachelor, she would wave me away impatiently. "In the old days, in Asia," she would say, "they burned up widows in husbands' funeral pyre." Then she would nod as though this explained everything, and quickly change the subject.

I dial Daniel Rollins's number quickly and almost hang up before I hear the clear, deep voice. "Hello?"

"Hello, Mr. Rollins. I'm sorry to bother you, but my name is Eleanor Shim. I'm Kyoung Ja's daughter."

There is a silence. I hear a long, hard breath.

"I just wanted to let you know that she died a couple of weeks ago. It was a heart attack and happened very suddenly."

"I know," he says after a pause. "I heard. From a mutual acquaintance. I'm sorry. My wife and I—"

"I've been going through her things. I found your letters."

There is another silence. "There were only the letters," he says finally. "I mean, we never... We only saw each other a few times. She was... your mother... I'm sorry if they upset you. I never meant—"

I twist the telephone cord around two fingers until my fingertips turn white from pressure.

"You knew my father?" I ask.

"Yes." Daniel Rollins sighs, low and long into my ear. "We worked on some research projects together. He was... a fine man, a good scientist."

"You know he died of a brain tumor? Inoperable? My mother nursed him for seven months."

"Yes, yes, I knew." His voice is scarcely audible.

"She was in love with you," I say, disbelieving. "All the time, she was in love with you."

"No," Daniel Rollins says. "She may have thought something like that, briefly. But her family was the most important thing to her."

I stare at the stack of letters on the desk in front of me, at my mother's name written in black ink above the address of the house where I am now sitting. "Was she really so unhappy?" I hear myself asking.

"I don't think so," Daniel Rollins says. "At least, no more than anyone." He sighs. "I'm sorry, Eleanor. This must be terrible for you. It's so impossible to explain. We never meant—"

I hold the receiver away from my ear and bring it down to the desk. A low moan comes from my throat, relieving a pressure in the hollow of my chest. I let it out and then suppress the others.

I feel pain like a poison spreading through my blood—like warmth, like illness. Tears fall, hot and bitter, onto the envelope in front of me, leaving puckered wet spots and blurring ink.

I sit on the back porch and listen to acorns falling on the roof, to the scurrying paws of a squirrel in mad pursuit. I am waiting for my husband and daughter to pick me up. Their faces, too, in a week of absence, have grown distant and unfocused in my memory. It is frightening how tenuous they seem. I am thinking how it was that I never questioned my mother's happiness. When I recall her mouth, it is a thin, determined line set against the violence of her task.

"Life is maintenance," she used to say. I took it as wisdom she meant to impart, a lesson she thought I must learn. I never considered that it was for herself she said it, the resolution she had come to.

Before we hung up, Daniel Rollins asked me to destroy his letters. "Please, if you wouldn't mind," he said. "They're ... well ... better gotten rid of. Your mother should never have kept them."

"She always kept everything," I said, and felt a sudden triumph of knowing. Daniel T. Rollins, whatever his claim on my mother, could not have known this. The things we keep, the secret and the mundane things, we keep at home.

Now I place the stack of letters on the counter. My mother's kitchen is blue and white with nothing on the countertops but matching canisters in diminishing sizes. I get a book of matches from a drawer; TIFFANY'S SEAFOOD is embossed across the turquoise cover. I light one of the matches and hold it over the sink; the flame burns my fingers. I drop it and it makes a faint hissing sound. I try again, strike another match and hold it, the letters safe in my other hand.

Stephen Dixon

August 1944—Beaver Lake—Derry, New Hampshire.
I'm the boy in the back row, extreme left. My sister Pat, then six,
is the girl with the short hair, four kids over from me in the back row.
Sitting in front of her is my sister Carole, age four, now deceased.
This was the entire camp—Miss Humphrey's camp it was called,
Miss Humphrey being the woman on the left. The woman on the
right, Molly O'Toole, gave me one of my first battles against anti-
Semitism; she called me a kike. I knew what the word meant and I
took her up on it, saying a Jew is as good as anybody else and it was
wrong for anyone, and especially an adult, to call someone that. For
my protest, I got a slap in the face that, like they say in some
nineteenth-century novels, I can still feel burning on my cheek.
I was in love, by the way, with Suzie, the girl standing beside my
sister Pat. She was Miss Humphrey's charge, smart as hell, and
never paid any attention to me in my two summers at the camp.

Stephen Dixon teaches in the Writing Seminars at Johns Hopkins University. *Long Made Short*, a collection of twelve post-*Frog* stories, will be published by Johns Hopkins University Press in September 1993. In early 1994, Henry Holt and Company will publish *The Selected Stories of Stephen Dixon*, containing sixty-five of Dixon's stories. His novel-in-progress, *Interstate* (from which "Interstate 3, Paragraph 2" is taken), will also be published by Henry Holt and Company, in late 1994.

STEPHEN DIXON
Interstate 3, Paragraph 2

heir car's still beside his. He took his mind off them a minute but there they are, probably never left. Doesn't look to see if the guy's staring or anything, just sees the front of their car even with his. Looks for a trooper car. Been looking on and off since he first felt those guys were menacing him and if one's around he'll pull over if it's on this side but first try to get their license plate number for he wants the cops to go after them now or when this is over, even if the plate's probably stolen or the car is for all he knows. But to get it he has to get behind them so he slows down, they slow down, maybe figuring what he wants to do, probably not. Oh yes, they know, they're old pros at all this stuff, he doesn't know anything about it or not much. But if a cop's across the road in the median what'll he do then? Car's got him blocked. Honk, that's what, honk like hell and open his window and wave and yell and slow down and stop on the shoulder and then back up on it if he's by that time far away from the cop or if he's near to get out fast and scream and wave for the cop, but get their plate number or much of it as he can and the state. Hasn't looked at them in a while now, feels weak at the wheel, for his kids not him, and wants to keep his eyes on the road and also on the front of their car in case he thinks they're going to bump or ram his, turns around quickly to the kids to see if they're all right and once through the rearview and that time doesn't see either of them. When a car or truck passes on the left in the speed lane he honks and honks but not once does the driver or passengers look at him when they're near, though the guy goes between facing front with a blank look as if innocent as hell or looking at him with a concerned one and once even saying or mouthing, "Anything wrong?" but a couple of passengers do look when they're way past and in one car two young boys in back point and he thinks look alarmed at him. He wants to roll down the window and yell out, "Help, stay near, help," while he continues honking, but by then they're way out of hearing range and he's also afraid of taking his hand off the wheel to roll down the window with the car next to him so close. Looks at the passenger window when no other cars are around and they've moved left a couple of feet and the guy's just staring at him with his fist holding up his chin as if he's studying his face hard and then he smiles almost politely and nicely and with his finger beckons to him. But to what, get his car even closer? Guy wants to say something to him? He crazy? And what's with the smile after all they've done and those hideous looks before? "Girls, you all right?" "Yes, we're all right, Daddy," Margo says. "We're playing by ourselves, why?" and he says, "Nothing, everything's fine. Still buckled up, though, right?" and she says, "Sure, us both. Why's that same car still there?" and he says, "Oh, nothing, they like our company I suppose or my good looks," guy smiling pleasantly at him, and she says, "They gay?" and he says, "Only kidding, honey, I know nothing about them." Then looks at the man again and he's beckoning with his finger but with this peculiar expression now, as if "Come into my dark chamber" or something, and moves the rearview around and sees both kids are busy with what they're doing with their eyes down and he looks at the man and he has that same peculiar expression but even more sinister or demonish, and turns front: this guy means trouble, they do, they're not letting up, they're sticking to him, slowing and speeding with him, getting their car even closer. Or maybe the guy's just a joker, a joker, that's all, driver the joker's friend, in on the joke and both just having fun by playing with him, and any accident that happens to the jokee or whatever you want to call him that goes along with the fun they couldn't give a single shit about. A car passes in the speed lane and he honks and honks and it goes even faster while he keeps his hand on the horn, guy looking front again, an angel. "Hey, you bastard," he wants to yell, "hey, stop, slow down, look over here," and open the window to yell it and wave but doesn't want to cause any thoughts that might upset the kids. Maybe what these guys want is to get him all the way into the slow lane and then force him off the shoulder into something, a ditch, or over it and down some hill, but why? Kicks. Kicks. Now they're in part of his lane he sees, no other cars around, and he has to move to the extreme right of it almost to the lane line. Doesn't want to get in the slow lane because then some more muscling by them and he's on the shoulder and whatever's there. Car behind him on the right honks, probably thinking he's switching lanes without signaling, and he honks and honks and the driver looks at him as she passes and he points to his left and mouths, "They're crazy, killers, they're nuts, maniacs, I need help, get help," and leans back so she can see through the front side windows and he doesn't look at the guy but figures he's doing what he did when the speeding car passed, facing front angelically, learned it sitting in church or school for when he did some lousy thing someone else got blamed for, and she scrunches up her face to a "Huh?" and shakes her head she doesn't get it and he points and mouths, "Those men, those men," and slits his throat with his finger several times and she signals left and cuts in front of him while he's honking like mad and more signaling to get in front of the men and then the speed lane, maybe because she's afraid of him, maybe she even gives the men a look she is when she's on the other side of them and the three cars are even. "What's wrong, Daddy?" Margo says and he says, "Why, my honking?" stopping now and Julie says, "Why were you?" and he says, "That stupid woman—that driver there, I mean, on the other side of the car next to us—well now she's away—but cutting in front of me without signaling, she could've killed us. All right, she wasn't that close, but it's the wrong thing to do," and Julie says, "Why, she should warn you, how?" and he says, "Lights, not lights but these signals," flicking the directionals up and down—the emergency lights, he thinks, turning them on—"but let's forget it, it upsets me but I'm okay," keeping his eyes on the road and front of their car, then the men, hoping that just with the emergency lights and his honking whenever he sees a truck or car, they'll drive away. Guy back to staring sinisterly at him. No other cars around, sees in the rearview and side mirrors. Nothing in front but that woman who's got to be doing eighty now. He speeds up but so does the car alongside, slows to sixty and they slow, looks at them and they're both laughing, looking at each other and him and back and forth like that and laughing and he thinks, What's so fucking funny? and mouths to the guy, "What's so funny?" and the guy points to him and he thinks, Me, huh, me, huh?—I'd like to shove your fucking laughs and smiles and teeth right down your dirty throats, you fucking idiots, get lost, get lost, and mouths, "I'm going to tell the police, do you hear me? the police," and the guy raises his shoulders so-o-o?, and he slows down some more, thinks he might pull into the slow lane, looks at the right sideview, no car there anywhere, guys' car slows down and driver honks and he looks and the guy opens his window and motions for him to open his and he thinks, What? and the guy mouths or says, "Open your window, open it," and again motions with his hand to and now his face isn't so bad, as if he only wants to tell him something like his door's open, wheel's low, and he says, "What?" and Julie says, "What, Dada?" and he says, "Not talking to you," and to the man, "What?" and the guy smiles nicely and drops his hand below the window and still smiling at him shouts, "You ... dumb ... prick," and hand comes up but with a gun in it and points it at him. "Holy shit," he yells, "holy God, kids, duck, get below," and to the man, "Don't, don't," and to the kids, "There's a guy with a gun in that car, duck, duck," and speeds and they speed and looks in the rearview and kids are shouting, "What, Daddy, what gun?" Margo, Julie, both, and he says, "Get below, the floor, on the floor, *floor!*" and swivels around, kids still on the seat, looking bewildered, scared, looks front and steering with his right hand,

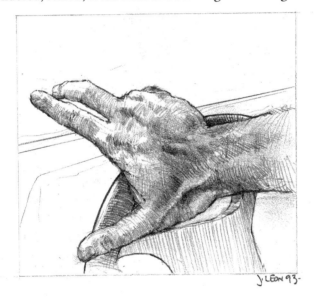

left reaches around his seat and gropes till it touches Margo's ankle and grabs it and jerks it down and shouts, "Unbuckle, get on the floor, both of you," jerking her leg down now, "maniacs in the next car, fucking maniacs, they'll kill us," and they start screaming and he yells, "Stop it, screaming, get down," and looks at the guys' car, he's too close to it and clamps both hands to the wheel and without signaling or looking pulls into the slow lane and they into the lane he left, and yells, "You hear me,

down, I'm saying, are you?—Margo!" and she says yes and he
yells, "Julie?" and Margo says yes and several cars in the speed
lanes now and he slows down and honks and the guys' car slows
and honks and he speeds up and they do, honking, blocking him
from any car's view and he shouts, "Oh no, what're we going
to do? keep down, down," and they're screaming and he thinks,
Think, come on, what should you do? oh my poor children, and
they're shouting, "Daddy" and some other things maybe not
words but they sound like them, "mudder foam, doll bait, pip
feed, call a thong, radiator so," and looks right, shoulder seems
fine to go on, thinks maybe with all the cars around the guy's
gun's gone, looks, barrel of it on the window bottom and aimed
at him, only the tip of it but enough to blow him to shit, same
crazy two-faced face and the guy saying or mouthing, "Hi, how
ya doing, great day, wouldn't you say?" driver busting a gut at
all this and pounding the dashboard while he steers with his left
hand and then no hands when he rips his hat off and whacks it
against the wheel, still plenty of room on the shoulder and he
drives onto it, try not to stop too suddenly and if the guys stop
in front of him, go in reverse fast as you can, and in back, the
reverse, go front and then try to shoot across the road without
getting clipped and onto the median if one's there, looks and
one's there, and then tear north and if they chase him, well, later,
if it happens, later but now stop, does, too suddenly, kids pitched
into his seat and he's thrown forward and back, guys go on but
then the crazy sticks his arm all the way out with the gun and
with his face behind it seems to be taking aim at them, and he
yells, "Kids, down, stay down," and dives to the seat and there's
gunshots, windshield shatters but doesn't break, screams in back
just before or just when the shots are fired and then, which one?
just Margo screaming. "Julie," he yells, "Julie, you okay? Margo,
you too? They're gone but both you stay down till I look."
Nothing from Julie. "Margo, tell me if you're all right." But the
men, and lifts his head just enough to see their car's not in front,

and turns around, they might've, but they couldn't've, but they might've gone on the median and around and then from behind and on the shoulder in back, and lifts his head above the seat but they're not there and jumps up on the seat and looks down and Margo's screaming and he yells, "Shush, tell me, come on, are you all right?" and she says, "Just my knees hurt from bumping the seat, but I think so," and he says, "You think you're otherwise okay?" quickly looking through all but the passenger-side windows to see that the men didn't come back and she says yes, rubbing her knees, and he says, "Julie," looking at her, on her side, no look back, "Julie, what about Julie?" and reaches down, can't reach her, that eye's closed and he thinks maybe she's unconscious, just her head hurt from hitting the seat, it's facing in that direction for that to happen, maybe she's otherwise okay, a cut and concussion but nothing much else, and Margo shrieks and says, "Daddy, there's blood," Julie doesn't stir, and he says, "Yours?" and she says, "I don't think so, it doesn't seem like I'm bleeding," and he says, "Check, check," and she feels herself all around and says, "I'm sure I'm not, not even my knees, they don't feel wet," and he leans over some more and stretches down to Julie, doesn't want to move her but has to to find out, should he get out of the car and go in the door where she is and do it that way? no, do it now, touches her but almost falls over and gets on the passenger seat and reaches down and lifts her up by an armpit till he can grab under both arms and lift her up straight, her legs stay on the floor, head flops around before settling, she doesn't seem to be breathing, there's blood on her neck and chin and coming through her sweater, and holding her around the back with one hand, unbuttons the top of her sweater and then her shirt and pulls down her undershirt soaked with blood, all the time saying, "Oh no, oh no," and thinking I know what it is, I don't want to know what it is, and screams when he sees blood running out of a bullet hole.

Lncle Hornbuckle.

LINDA HORNBUCKLE

Blues singer

Interview

by Linda Davies

Linda Hornbuckle sings gospel, pop, Motown, and blues and has worked with such groups as Quarterflash and Body and Soul. She is currently lead singer with the No Delay Band and last fall was named best female vocalist by the Portland Music Association and the Cascade Blues Association.

Linda Hornbuckle

DAVIES: *I understand you're a two-career person.*

HORNBUCKLE: Yes. I work at a day-care center during the day. Since I work late, I go in at ten-thirty or eleven every morning and make lunch for forty little kids. After their naps, we chat about the day and what they've learned. I try to enhance whatever they've studied that day so they don't forget it, because it goes away fast. We try to really get it in them, you know,

"What number did you learn today?" and, "What letter did you learn today? Let's go over this again. Tell me about it. I want to know what was exciting in class today." They're so young, and when they make the first letter of their day, they think it's the *coolest* thing. Yesterday, I was working with this little boy—his name is Edward—and we made a giant *E*. He showed his dad, "Lookit! Look what I did!" And his dad was excited. Edward's three years old, and maybe by the time he leaves day-care, he'll even write his whole name—and maybe a couple of other things, you know, *Mom, love,* make a heart, just little things like that.

That's exciting for a kid. Kids didn't do such things so early when I was little. The rural area I lived in didn't even have a kindergarten at that time.

The way society is now, they need a big jump. I think the thing is to get them geared into going to kindergarten, going to elementary school, going to high school, going to *college.* To let them know these are the things you have to do in order to make yourself a better person. "Mom and Dad get up and go to work. I get up and go to school so I can learn how to be like Mom and Dad."

So how is singing like working with kids?

I give a lot of myself. I try to be picky about what I sing and if I can't relate to it, I won't do it. If the lyrics aren't going to be resolved and give me strength at the end of it, I won't do it. I like sad stories, but I like the outcome to be totally fantastic. I want people to leave feeling like they took something with them, like I made them feel something. It's important to me to make them feel like I wasn't out here just to be out here. I want you to feel some of this pain I went through, some of the happiness I've gone through, and to go out thinking tomorrow's going to be a better day.

Do you think many singers think that way?

I don't know. *I* do. I think you're here to do something—

whether you're a writer, or an athlete, or a mom, or just a person. You're here to do something and you have to give in order to feel good.

Is that something that comes, to some degree, from your background, from growing up in a church environment?

I think that has a lot to do with it. But as far back as I can remember, I was always giving. I remember putting my dolls to bed because I didn't want them to be out in the cold. I'd cover them up or sleep with them.

So that's just part of you.

With music, it's a passion for me. When you're singing about pain, *show* the pain. I've had some pain in my life, and you've got to go through all those areas. You can't just ignore them. That's not me; I'm not like that. I like getting my message across—I guess that's what I'm trying to say.

I think that your investment, your involvement, in your singing—aside from the fact that your voice is magnificent—is what lets you grab people off their seats and have them think that you're singing to them, personally. This winter, at the Oregon Women in the Arts festival, I think the audience would have listened to you all night. You didn't actually sing very long.

I was told I only had a couple of minutes. The program was so long, and I didn't want to just wail, wail, wail away and bore everybody. That was a strange night. I had been stuck in the elevator for about half an hour before the show with ten or fifteen other people, including my sisters and an elderly lady who was claustrophobic and had a heart problem. We had to make room to lay her down and calm her down. She said, "Sing. Sing to me." So we sang, and she calmed down. We all went through a lot that night! It was just good to get out and watch the show, to watch these great women.

When we went for the photo for the *Oregonian,* there was so much energy in the room. I hope we do this again and that we have time to socialize and really get to know each other because they were very, very powerful. It made me feel good that people thought that I was one of these women. It was a great show. I enjoyed *watching* the show.

You were able to watch the show even though you hadn't performed yet? You weren't nervous?

Well, I was so small when I started, and I was very religious— I still am, but I'm just not so structured—and I learned that when you're giving thanks to God, you're not to be shy with him, you're supposed to really show him love.

Well, you give a lovely gift to your audience.

It *is* a gift. When I was four or five years old, I had a bad stuttering problem and I couldn't even say "daddy"; it was so hard for me to say "daddy." My parents took me to an evangelist and he prayed for me, and it went away.

No!

Yes, it just went away.

Wow. Do you ever wonder what to think about things like that?

Maybe you need a push. Maybe you need somebody to feel like you can do this, and make you believe *I can do this.* I believe very much in God. I believe that he helps us and I believe that he gives us different things to do. He doesn't do everything for you. Some things you have to get up and do for yourself.

I took an interest in music at an early age. I would turn off all the Motown and pop stuff, and I would go to something really soft and nice. I still like them today; I like doing the slow, sweet things.

My dad was into country and western. I think we were the only black people in northeast Portland who listened to that. He'd take us to school and we'd say, "Da-ad! Turn that down— please—we're getting close to school! Turn it down!"

But in Oregon and Portland at that time, there wasn't a black gospel station, and country-western were the only people who would do "Amazing Grace" or "Will the Circle Be Unbroken?"

and he likes to listen to them. I grew up to appreciate it. He said,
"You should listen to *all* music. You can learn from all of it."

I don't try to limit myself. Except for rap. I can't get into that,
for some reason. My niece will say, "Have you heard this? Can
you do this?"

And I say, "No, I don't think so. It's good for you, but not for
me." But I like some of it. I like the good messages, talking about
issues. "Why? Why are the police on me? Why is this stuff going
on?" You have to go out and get what you want. You can sit
around and rap all day long, but you've got to go get what you
want. I don't care who you are, you can't be afraid. You've got
to go for what you know, and even if you fail, you pick up and
go again.

How did you learn that?

My dad. He's just one of those people who's not scared of life,
of anything. He's just out there.

How has that affected your music?

Oh, God. When I first started singing [outside of church] with
Lovin' from the Oven, we were a house band for three years.
And we decided it was time to venture out. It was just down to
Albany, Oregon, and to Longview, Washington, but I'm
thinking I'm going on a long trip, you know. When we got to
Longview, we were at a little bar called Bart's. I'm expecting this
huge crowd of people like always, being Miss Princess, or
whatever, on the stage, and here it's a hole-in-the-wall, ceiling
falling down, and there are these loggers who've probably never
seen black people at all—and they're throwing ice at us!

Are you kidding me?

No, seriously. I was very, very lucky to be with great guys.
They were so protective. When I was first starting, they came by
to meet my father. I don't know what they discussed with my
dad; I never asked him or them.

I should back up. At first, Daddy was totally not into this. I
snuck around and I snuck out. I wasn't supposed to be doing this;

I was supposed to be singing in church.

That was tough, I bet.

Yeah, because I didn't want to hurt him, but I was compelled to do something that I wanted to do really bad. Finally, he came to me and he told me, "Well, this is what you decided to do?"

And I said, "Yes." This was the most heart-to-heart talk we'd ever had. We'd had talks before, but not like this.

He said, "Well, I want you to know that I'm going to pray for you that you be safe." And I think that's why I've been safe all these years. I was—what—twenty-two, green, out of church, didn't know anything, didn't drink, didn't do anything.

Pretty vulnerable.

Yeah—pretty stupid. I was curious, more than anything. I remember calling home, crying. All he said was, "Well Linda, you made the decision. You have to make your decisions. I'm always here for you, but I can't tell you what to do. I can't tell you to keep on, and I can't tell you to come back. This is what you have to do."

I kept truckin' at it, and it got better. I learned how to handle the drunks and the men and the drugs and the alcohol—all of it—and not let it get the best of me. And I think most of it was his prayers—and mine, too, I guess. And being with good people who cared about me.

I'm happy with myself and the way I feel about God. I think I would like being closer to him. As far as the order of services and the way I was brought up, I should probably be there more, but right now, I'm content. I think he's with me all the time. I don't dwell on it. When I need to go to church, I go. Sometimes I wake up on Sunday morning and look at my boyfriend Mark and say, "I gotta go to church." I go listen to the choir sing, or get up with them and sing, or listen to Daddy preach, or testimony. And it's something I needed to hear that day. It's something I have to keep close to me, try to keep inside of me all the time, to keep me straight. But it's an individual thing. It's not up to me to decide what religion is right or who's wrong. I really admire my dad for that. He never said, "Oh, you can't go to the Catholic church 'cause they're wrong. You can't go to the Baptist church 'cause they're wrong." He never said that. He's always been open.

Really? I have to admit that I never thought the Pentecostal church had much room for other points of view.

No. Our church is Pentecostal, and my dad never taught us to downfall anybody. People worship in different ways in different parts of the world.

Malcolm—when I went to go see *X*— he was convinced that white people were terrible and we should all move back to Africa. When he went over there and saw black Muslims, white Muslims, Japanese Muslims, all kinds of people—he was flabbergasted. With his lifestyle and the things he went through when he was younger—it was so beautiful to see the outcome of it.

I'm embarrassed to say I didn't know much about Malcolm X until recently.

I was taught that he was racist and militant, and Martin Luther King was the person I was supposed to find out about.

You and me both. I was born in New York, but did most of my growing up in southern Oregon, which is very, very white. I understand there was even a sundown law until 1962.

Oh yes. I remember singing in Coos Bay and a guy walked in with a Klan outfit on.

Really? When did that happen?

Early seventies.

Were you terrified?

I was. I thought we were going to die. It was an experience. The guys in the band just said that we weren't going to start till he left, and he did. But there were nice people there, too, who even invited us to stay in their home.

When you were growing up, did your parents warn you to be careful of white people?

The only time I remember is when we took a trip down South when I was seven or eight. We stopped in Kansas to wash clothes, and I guess we were on the wrong side of town. The state police came and told us we couldn't be there. This was in the sixties, and we *weren't* supposed to be there, and my dad didn't care. I remember he had taken his shirt off to wash it and his arms were folded while the cop was talking to him, and he says, "I'm not leaving here till my clothes are done." And we finished our laundry and they followed us till we got out of the state.

How did you feel?

I felt a lot of fear. I didn't really know what was happening because up here in Oregon, you know, we had a white family across the street from us and one alongside of us. This was totally foreign to me.

When we actually got down South, that was another culture shock—seeing all the black people, you know.

Why?

Well, because there were no white people around. And the way the black people lived. My grandma had outside plumbing and chickens running around. Driving around in the country with no streetlights, but they knew where they were going—that was fascinating to me. And people were just super, super poor. I went to a great aunt and uncle's house where all they had was a piano and a bed—a hall and two rooms. That was it.

A piano?

Yes, but with not very many keys on it. Another aunt's house reminded me of a fairy tale because it was one of those tiny places way off in the woods with a little light on and smoke coming from the chimney. When you got inside, it was so warm and there were all these homemade dolls and homemade food. She was severely cross-eyed and kind of round and very jolly and loving. Her name was Aunt Mary. I remember her so well!

And these were relatives you'd never met before?

I'd never met in my life. I remember cousins. My mom's cousin lived in a little shack. I think she was kind of off, I don't know, my mom would probably disagree with me. But when we got there, she said, "Well, how ya doin'?" and after she had gabbed with my mom for a little while, she said, "Let's go look at the graves!" And ten feet from the house there were all these relatives—lined up—outside the house. At that age I didn't want to go to any graveyard. No way!

A different world altogether.

And that's where my parents grew up. They're so funny! They knew each other when they were children. They used to, like, fight each other. My dad would chase Mom all over the place! He said one time he chased her down to the creek and he jumped over a rattlesnake, trying to catch her. They used to have feuds and stuff. It's a true story. You see why I'm crazy. They've got too many stories for me! Grandma used to tell us about storms, "Oh, it took your uncle Sudd and carried him across the way!"

And I guess that stuff happens. You know, tornadoes and cyclones were prevalent and they *would* take your house away and you'd have to build your house up again the next day. I don't think my dad wanted us to grow up down there like that. I just think that he thought it'd be easier here. He wanted better for us. He didn't want us to deal with all the racism.

What are your professional goals?

Well, gosh, I guess I'm like everybody else. I want an album. I want it to be successful. I want to travel. I want to turn on the radio or go to the record store and see a CD of me. I want to make my mark. I think I'm ready. How does Mark say it?— "You're ripe. You're ready to go out there." I want it to happen. I want it bad.

Are there things in your way, or is it a road that you just have to keep charging on?

There's nothing in my way. I'm the only thing in my way.

And you're getting out of your own way? That's what closing in on forty does to a person, isn't it?

Well, yeah. Forty and a bad marriage and all that stuff. You become stagnant and you don't want to pull this shit anymore. You come to the realization that it's time. I have to do it now. Get out of my road.

When you are up there singing, you radiate. I would guess that is one of the times you feel the most alive. Is that true?

Gosh, I don't think about that. I do *feel* radiant. It's almost like a contest. They're here to listen because they want to see what people are talking about, you know? It becomes a challenge every time. I always feel like I have to *make* people listen. Maybe that's why it comes out the way it does. Especially when people are talking, having their conversations. It's real annoying to me because I want them to listen to what I'm doing. And I think, I'm going to *make* you stop talking and listen to me. And that's what I try to do.

Well, you do make them listen.

Sometimes I'm lucky, and sometimes I'm not.

Keeps you working.

Yeah, because you don't win every night. But they pay to come see you and you've got to put on a show. And you have to make them feel at home. That's very important, to make them feel like: This is my living room, or, I feel like it's my living room and I want you to be comfy. I want you to sit back and relax and let me drive you to oblivion, or wherever. I try. It's on me.

You're very gracious, very generous with your audience.

I try to be myself. It comes from my heart, from my center.

Were you too young to remember when your parents started their church?

Actually, no. There were some things going on in the organization that my dad was involved in that made him feel that he was called to do something on his own, to start his own, to get his own flock. He felt he was compelled to go do this. He was criticized. He was kicked out of the organization. The bishop told people not to go to his church.

It was very rough. He had stopped work to be a full-time minister. I remember, for a month, he was shut in a closet. I don't know if he was shut in all day, or what, but I remember him praying in his closet for hours at a time—meditating and praying. Just by himself.

I remember nobody being there at our church. It was a storefront church, on Williams Avenue, and it was next to a church building with a steeple and all the proper things. And we had this little, ugly, storefront church next to it. But gradually people came—and left—and they came—and they left—it just went on. His ministry has been like that; people have come and gone. He's never had a full house. He's never complained about it. He's always been grateful for what he has had.

Whenever we went to visit or to sing anywhere where he was to preach, I would always sing before he got up—it was always something real spiritual with us. I was very close to him, and I used to watch him a lot.

From the time I was small, I think I knew his pain from that. I think that's why I give so much— because I want these people to know my daddy's good, he's not bad. I kind of felt his pain and I tried to relieve it through song.

I remember one day at a prayer meeting, I was crying. I was really small. I remember him coming down and holding me and hugging me. It was such a safeness, like everything was going to be okay.

When you were growing up, what life did you expect you'd be living when you were thirty-eight years old?

I thought I'd have an album out by now.

When you were a kid, you thought this?

Uh-huh. When I first started singing, I thought it wouldn't take very long. It takes a lot longer than you'd think!

So you've always planned on being a singer.

Yes, as far back as I can remember.

What would be the greatest risk you could take in your music?

Abandoning it.

What would happen to you?

There have been periods of time that I stopped and didn't do it for a while, and I'd find myself to be bored and mean. I knew what was wrong with me, I needed to go sing. I was in a pretty abusive relationship. All I was interested in was making this man happy. Trying to be strong for him. I thought I wasn't going to do anything with this music anyway, so I'd just get a job and work and be cool and not worry about it. It was the most miserable time in my life, and I didn't realize it till I got out of the situation and looked back at it. Even to this day, I can't believe I did that. It's like a piece of my life was just thrown away.

What did you gain from it?

Nothing.

Nothing?

Nothing, except knowing not to do it again.

I had this thing about being able to help—I could change this person. I could make this person a better person. Did not work. That person is the same way today, and he could care less about changing or being different. I could have done this my whole life, and it wouldn't have changed a thing. Since I got rid of him, things just shot up! It's been remarkable.

What emotion makes your voice come out the most powerfully?

Pain. I do it well. I can sing about pain. I also like to make the pain go away at the end of the song, so it doesn't leave you suffering. I want it to make you feel better before it's over. I mean, make you feel wonderful.

Thank you so much, Linda.

Susan Burmeister

SUSAN BURMEISTER
The Two-Step

I hate it when you look at me like that. Like you're just waiting for me to say something else, something you can make sense of. This is as clear as I get, Jerry. This is just as straight and simple as I get." Paula threw her arms open wide as if that would make him see.

With her arms like that and her head off to the side, she was like some crazy Christ-figure. Jerry looked at her for a moment, reviewing what she'd said, and then realized he was doing exactly what she had just accused him of. It didn't seem like a fault. Waiting for all the facts, waiting until he understood, that struck him as highly sensible. Leaping to conclusions, acting hastily, now that would be a fault. He was going over all this in his mind when he heard Paula stamping her feet.

"Answer me. What are you thinking? What do you think of what I've been saying?" She slapped her hand on the counter. "Are you even listening?" She slapped it again. "Say something!"

Jerry went over to the sink and turned on the faucet, holding his hand under it until he felt it get cold. He got a glass from the cupboard and filled it, drank it down, and filled it again.

"Why is it, Jerry, that whenever I am trying to talk to you, whenever we are trying to actually talk, you get so thirsty? And let's see," Paula pulled up her sleeve and looked at the time, "in about twenty minutes, you'll have to go piss it all and you'll take ten minutes in the bathroom doing that. The only time you ever wash your hands after is when we're fighting." Disgust narrowed her eyes and pushed in the corners of her mouth. "This time, Jerry, *this* time I'm coming in with you. We'll stand in there together and drop our drawers. Oh, that's right. You don't drop your drawers. You just whip it out and aim. More or less aim, anyway."

These nasty turns always surprised him. Tracing back over the fights they'd had recently, he could identify the precise statements Paula had made each time: "Your breath, Jerry, is atrocious. You're just one big stinkball, head to toe, aren't you?" "Do you actually have any friends? I mean real friends? People who *want* to be with you? I don't think so." "You're big, Jerry. You're big and strong, at least what hasn't gone to flab. But I guess that's about all you've got going for you anymore, isn't it? Your bigness?" "Your idea of great sex and my idea of great sex are not remotely related. Not even *remotely*." He never heard his name said so often as she said it during these tirades. She made it sound as if it tasted bad and she couldn't quite shake loose of it. Like a dog with a hairball in its mouth.

He drank down his second glass, then leaned back against the kitchen counter, legs crossed at the ankle, arms crossed low on his stomach, watching to see what she would do next.

"This was not what I had in mind when I got married, Jerry. Not at all. If I had known, I would never have said yes. Never in a million years. Wait a minute. That's right. You never did really say the words, did you? You never actually came out and said, 'Will you marry me?' It just happened. One thing led to another and we were walking down the aisle. Wasn't that how it went? I don't know what I was thinking of. I can't imagine."

Paula walked across the kitchen and stood in front of him, nodding slowly. "Why don't you ask me again, Jerry? Why don't you come on out with it; do it right this time and say the

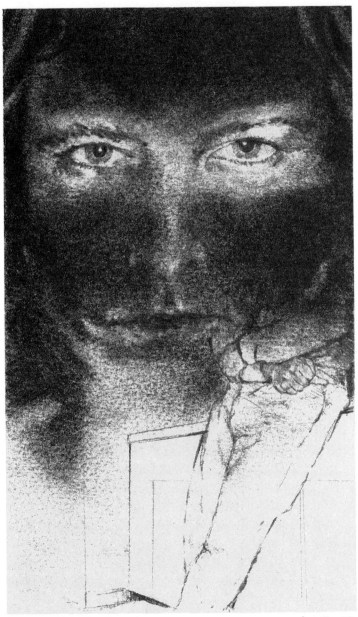

words. Say them, Jerry. Say, 'Will you marry me?' " Paula mouthed the words a second time, inches from his face. "And this time, *this* time I'll get it right. This time I'll say, 'What a fuckin' *joke.*' "

He felt his right arm twitch, and held himself in check. Paula noted this, and half her mouth smiled as she turned and looked out the window, shaking her head. "You can't even—" His fist leapt out from his crossed arms and planted hard on Paula's jaw, cracking her sentence in half, knocking the words off her tongue for the first time in too long.

Jerry stood over her there in the kitchen, breath coming hard, his hands fisted and ready at his sides, an emancipated man.

"Will. You. Marry. Me," he said at last.

$\mathcal{S}$TORIES GONE BY

Past issues are available for $11 each.

Joyce Thompson
Sports Cars

Abigail Thomas
Just Married 1960

Mary McGarry Morris
The Perfect Tenant

Wayne Johnson
On the Observation Car

R. Kevin Maler
Counterfeit

Marilyn Krysl
Extinct Species

WINTER 1992
Issue 1

Mary O'Dell
Yellow Pages

Anndee Hochman
Dark Is Not a Single Shade of Gray

Sigrid Nunez
Italies

Susan Burmeister
Steps to Goodness

Interviews with Patrick Tierney, street poet, and Gerard Byrne, painter, both from Dublin. Celia Wren on writers in South Africa.

༄

Christopher Woods
Today, Quite Early

Abigail Thomas
Babysitting

Jack Cady
Tinker

Rosina Lippi-Green
Letters from Vienna

Gregory McNamee
The First Emperor

Corinne Demas Bliss
In the Perfect Privacy of His Own Mind

Lily King
Up in Ontario

SPRING 1992
Issue 2

Valerie Block
Java

Kathleen Tyau
How to Cook Rice

David Huddle
Reunion Joke

Stephen Dixon
The Stranded Man

Susan Burmeister
Second Tuesday

Interview with Portland artist Dennis Clemmens and interview with/article by Maina wa Kinyatti, a writer in exile.

༄

Stan Rogal
Skin Deep

Daniel Wallace
My Old Vanity

Barbara Bechtold
Nushka

David Haynes
Busted

Marilyn Krysl
The Hiroshima Maiden

Elizabeth Inness-Brown
The Surgeon

Amy Selwyn
Mims

SUMMER 1992
Issue 3

Celia Wren
Liberation

Louis Gallo
Dead by Tuesday

Kyle Ann Bates
How It Is

Evelyn Sharenov
Magic Affinities

Susan Burmeister
Kites

Interviews with actress Vana O'Brien, and Siobhan Dowd, program director of PEN's Freedom-to-Write. Article by Siobhan Dowd, *Writer Detained: Maria Elena Cruz Varela.*

༄

Janice Rosenberg
Chance of a Lifetime

Cathie Beck
Español

Terry Wolverton
A Whisper in the Veins

Joyce Thompson
First Day of School

Ed Weyhing
How Do You Know?

A. Manette Ansay
The Wallet

FALL 1992
Issue 4

Jack Holland
The Yard

Eileen McGuire
Inhale, Exhale

Mary Ellis
Wings

Stephen Dixon
Many Janes

Susan Burmeister
Pressing Tight

Interviews with writers Carolyn Chute and Stephen Dixon. Article by Siobhan Dowd, *Writer Detained: Thiagarajah Selvanithy.*

$\mathcal{S}$TORIES GONE BY

Gary D. Wilson
What Happens Instead

Mary Ellis
Angel

Robert Abel
Prized Possessions

Lawson Fusao Inada
The Flower Girls

Lee Martin
Secrets

Sigrid Nunez
The Loneliest Feeling in the World

WINTER 1993
Issue 5

Elizabeth Judd
Mirrors to the Soul

James English
Goosewing

Susan J. Alenick
Chips and Whetstones

Susan Burmeister
Man across the Aisle

Interviews with writers
William Styron and Joyce Thompson.
Article by Siobhan Dowd,
Writer Detained: Gustavo Guzman.

Floyd Skloot
The Royal Family

Marina Harris
Skin Tailoring

Joyce Thompson
Who Lives in the Basement

Libby Schmais
Losses

Louis Gallo
And the Greatest of These

Daniel Gabriel
In the House of Mr. Poo

SPRING 1993
Issue 6

Stephen Dixon
Hand

Peter Gordon
The Net

Danit Brown
Breathing

Wayne Karlin
Dov's Toes

Susan Burmeister
When Lila Comes Home

Interview with writer Anne Rice and
Glimmer Train illustrator, Jon Leon.
Article by Siobhan Dowd,
Writer Detained:
Mansur Muhammad Ahmad Rajih

What do they have going now?

"I'm a little surprised at your moral fiber, sister," he said. "That you'd not show more commitment in front of the youngster." His face was getting red again, and spit was forming at the edge of his mouth.

from "Empty Gesture" by Ed Weyhing

Though I had taken Virginia to be a woman content with occasional company and conversation, which I had supplied her with these last few weeks, I realized this was only true to a point, that point having been reached that very evening ... There on the seat cushion was a key hooked to a piece of green oblong plastic with the number 214 written on it.

from "The Main Thing" by Daniel Wallace

It always seems to me that there's something slightly artificial about mountaineering writing, because whenever someone is suspended like a fly on that vertical face, you always know that on the other side of that mountain is a path with a signpost.

from an interview with Jonathan Raban by Michael Upchurch

Not that any of us in the kitchen will actually get around to reading *Iron John,* although I have looked up the story in Grimms. Iron Hans — the German equivalent of Iron Johnny, which puts a whole other light on it, doesn't it? I mean, Iron Johnny? It's like being lectured on the Equal Rights Amendment by someone named Tiffany.

from "Gulf Wars" by Frances Kuffel